Looking up, I saw that Linnsy had been attacked by a strange vine. Its thick tendrils had wrapped themselves around her legs. Weird orange pods were creeping toward her, making a terrible sucking sound as they approached.

Linnsy struck at them. They flinched, drawing back some two or three feet. But at the same time one of them spit a wad of steaming purple fluid that just missed her face.

Before I could think of what to do, I heard a cry of rage from Tim. He ran toward the vine, brandishing a piece of metal. I realized he must have wrenched it from the wreckage of the ship.

"Stop it!" he screamed, hacking at the vine. "Stop it! Stop it! *Stop it!*"

Books by Bruce Coville

The A.I. Gang Trilogy
Operation Sherlock
Robot Trouble
Forever Begins Tomorrow

Bruce Coville's Alien Adventures
Aliens Ate My Homework
I Left My Sneakers in Dimension X
The Search for Snout
Aliens Stole My Body

Camp Haunted Hills
How I Survived My Summer Vacation
Some of My Best Friends Are Monsters
The Dinosaur That Followed Me Home

I Was a Sixth Grade Alien
I Was a Sixth Grade Alien
The Attack of the Two-Inch Teacher
I Lost My Grandfather's Brain
Peanut Butter Lover Boy
Zombies of the Science Fair
Don't Fry My Veeblax!
Too Many Aliens
Snatched from Earth

Magic Shop Books
Jennifer Murdley's Toad
Jeremy Thatcher, Dragon Hatcher
The Monster's Ring
The Skull of Truth

My Teacher Books
My Teacher Is an Alien
My Teacher Fried My Brains
My Teacher Glows in the Dark
My Teacher Flunked the Planet

Space Brat Books
  Space Brat
  Space Brat 2: Blork's Evil Twin
  Space Brat 3: The Wrath of Squat
  Space Brat 4: Planet of the Dips
  Space Brat 5: The Saber-toothed Poodnoobie

The Dragonslayers
Goblins in the Castle
Monster of the Year
The World's Worst Fairy Godmother

Available from MINSTREL Books

Bruce Coville's Chamber of Horrors
  #1 Amulet of Doom
  #2 Spirits and Spells
  #3 Eyes of the Tarot
  #4 Waiting Spirits

Oddly Enough
Space Station Ice-3

Available from ARCHWAY Paperbacks

BRUCE COVILLE

SNATCHED FROM EARTH

Illustrated by Tony Sansevero

A MINSTREL® BOOK

Published by POCKET BOOKS
New York   London   Toronto   Sydney   Singapore

A MINSTREL PAPERBACK *Original*

A Minstrel Book published by
POCKET BOOKS, a division of Simon & Schuster, Inc.
1230 Avenue of the Americas, New York, NY 10020

© 2000 Fox Family Properties, Inc.
Fox Family and the Family Channel name and logo are the
respective trademarks of Fox and I.F.E., Inc. All Rights Reserved.

Text copyright © 2000 by Bruce Coville
Illustrations copyright © 2000 by Tony Sansevero

ISBN: 0-671-02657-7

First Minstrel Books printing September 2000

10 9 8 7 6 5 4 3 2 1

A MINSTREL BOOK and colophon are registered trademarks of
Simon & Schuster, Inc.

YTV is a registered trademark of YTV Canada, Inc.
© 2000 YTV Canada, Inc.
A Corus™ Entertainment Company

Cover art by Miro Sinovcic

Printed in the U.S.A.

For
Seaton McLean and Ted Riley,
Visionaries

CHAPTER
1
[TIM]

Stowaways

It's late, and the others are asleep.

Judge Wingler's assistant came in a while ago to pick up the material we had already written, all the chapters telling how we first got involved in what the galactic media are calling "The Earth Based Catastrophe that Nearly Ended Life as We Know It."

I would have liked more time to work on my chapters. I was completely honest about how upset I was when Pleskit's friend Maktel came to earth for a visit, but I'm afraid I didn't sound very mature.

On the other hand, given what happened to

Linnsy, maybe it's just as well I'm not all that mature. If I was, I might be in her situation right now.

The weird thing is, sometimes I almost wish I were.

The pages we had finished covered the first half of the story, beginning from the time Maktel arrived on Earth from Hevi-Hevi for a visit with Pleskit and started driving me nuts. They talked about our suspicions regarding Ellico *vec* Bur, the strange two-part being who arrived on the same ship with Maktel to visit Pleskit's Fatherly One, Meenom Ventrah. We had gotten right up to the point where Pleskit, Maktel, Linnsy, and I sneaked onto Ellico *vec* Bur's ship to see if we could find any clues to what the Trader(s) were up to.

I still remember the horror I felt when Ellico *vec* Bur came aboard. We quickly hid in a storage space, hoping the Trader(s) would leave before they found us.

They left all right, but not in the way we expected. They blasted off and left the planet—with the four of us still hiding on the ship! I have always wanted to go into space, but I never planned on making the trip by being snatched from Earth by someone(s) who seemed to be total villains.

I'm too wound up to sleep. I guess I might as well keep writing.

It was pitch black in the storage room until Pleskit's *sphen-gnut-ksher* began to spark. Its purple light illuminated the terrified faces of my companions.

Linnsy was standing directly to my right. I felt bad that she had gotten dragged into this mess—though if I had a choice of who I'd want to have by my side when I was in trouble, she would be the one.

Next to her stood Pleskit himself, his pet Veeblax clinging to his shoulder. I could tell the little animal was as scared as I was, since it couldn't choose a shape to settle in, but kept shifting from one form to another.

Next to Pleskit was Maktel, his pudgy face wide-eyed in horror.

I wondered if I looked as frightened as he did. I sure felt that way.

"What are we going to do, guys?" whispered Linnsy.

I've known Linnsy since before kindergarten, so I could tell how hard she was working to keep the quaver out of her voice. Her nervousness increased the fear wringing my own gut. I realized it was possible we might never see Earth again.

Earth? Heck, I wasn't sure we would live to see another *day* once Ellico *vec* Bur found out we were aboard.

"This is all your fault, Maktel," said Pleskit bitterly. "If you hadn't insisted on checking Ellico *vec* Bur's ship, we would still be back at the embassy with the rest of the class, enjoying the party."

"And if you had believed my suspicions to begin with, I would not have needed to insist on that checking," replied Maktel, sounding equally bitter. "I did say those Trader(s) were up to something, didn't I?"

"Actually, we still don't know if they're up to anything," I pointed out.

"Stay out of this, Tim!" snapped Pleskit, which was so totally unlike him that I blinked and took a step back. I might have backed up more, but one step was as far as I could go into the tiny chamber we were trapped in.

Of course, in a way I had been feeling trapped ever since Maktel arrived from Hevi-Hevi—trapped by the nagging fear in my gut that I would be left out of things when he and Pleskit got back together.

Well, I'd managed to keep myself included—and look where it had gotten me!

A sudden movement at my shoulder distracted me. I put a protective hand on the mesh pouch I wore there. Inside the pouch was a "purple pickle" that, with luck and proper care, might turn into a Veeblax like Pleskit's. I suddenly wondered if the stress of blasting off would be bad for it.

"This won't hurt the *oog-slama*, will it?" I asked nervously.

Maktel puffed out his cheeks in a Hevi-Hevian sign of exasperation. "By the Seven Moons of Skatwag!" he snapped. "We've got more to worry about than that stupid Veeblax in the making!"

"Will you shut up!" I hissed. I kept my voice low so that Ellico *vec* Bur wouldn't hear us—

then remembered that the Trader(s) couldn't hear us anyway, since the room was sound-proof.

Maktel looked at me angrily.

His *sphen-gnut-ksher* began to spark.

I pressed myself to the wall, wondering if he was about to zap me.

CHAPTER
2
[LINNSY]

Way-outward Bound

I couldn't believe Tim and Maktel were about to get into a fight. What a totally boy thing to do—waste time fighting when what we really needed to do was figure out how we were going to survive!

It made me wonder if males are the same everywhere in the galaxy.

"All right, that's enough," I said sternly, stepping between them. "You, too, Pleskit. I don't care whose fault this is, or how stupid each of you thinks the other is. What I want to know is: What are we going to do now?"

Pleskit blinked. "Sorry, Linnsy," he said

7

softly. "You are correct. I was exhibiting inappropriate behavior."

I was so surprised I probably would have fallen over, if there had been enough room. Obviously males across the galaxy were not *all* alike. I can't imagine any Earthling guy I know settling down so quickly—much less apologizing that way.

"You and Pleskit are correct," Maktel said, bowing his head. "I apologize for my sharp tongue."

Tim looked from one to the other, then back again. He closed his eyes and shook his head, as if trying to make sense of this. "Uh, I'm sorry, too," he said at last. Then, quickly, as if he found the act of apologizing supremely uncomfortable, he said, "Okay, let's try to think. What do we actually know about our situation?"

"Well, we know that Ellico *vec* Bur have kidnapped us for nefarious reasons of their own," said Maktel.

"Actually, we don't even know that," said Pleskit mildly.

"What are you talking about?" cried Maktel. "Didn't they just snatch us into space?"

"They certainly did," said Pleskit. "But did they do that on purpose, or did we just happen to be aboard when they took off? The real question right now is, do we try to let them know we're here, or do we wait until the ship lands and try to sneak away, hoping we can find some way to get back home?"

This was a tough one. The longer we delayed letting the Trader(s) know we were on board, the farther we got from Earth. But if we did manage to let them know, who was to say they wouldn't just zap us, or fling us into space, or something?

When I brought this point up, Pleskit said, "I'm sure they are far too civilized for that."

"Pleskit, you are a dreamer," said Maktel, shaking his head. "The members of the Trading Federation are not as universally upright and moral as you would like to think."

"Based on our experiences since you came to Earth, I'd have to say Maktel is right," said Tim. I had to give him credit for saying that, since I knew it would gall him to admit Maktel was right about anything, much less take his side in a dispute with Pleskit.

"Let me check something," said Pleskit. He went to the door of the little room where we were hidden. When he turned back, his face was grim. "We're still locked in. I had hoped that once takeoff was complete, the lock would do an automatic release."

"So we couldn't tell Ellico *vec* Bur we're here even if we wanted to," I said. "All right, what do we do instead?"

"Let's start by listing what we know," said Tim.

Unfortunately, the answer to this question turned out to be: almost nothing. Sure, Ellico *vec* Bur were a suspicious twosome, and Maktel was convinced they were involved in some horrible plot. But if so, what was it? Not to mention: Where were we going—and how long would it take to get there?

I glanced at my watch. It had been fifteen minutes since we took off.

"Don't count on that for an accurate display of time," said Maktel. "The ship is going fast enough by now that time will be passing differently for us than it does back on the planet."

I knew—mostly from Tim babbling about his science-fiction shows—that the closer you get to the speed of light, the slower time actually passes for you. But I hadn't really thought about that weirdosity applying to us.

"How much time has really gone by back on Earth?" I asked, feeling a new surge of panic as I wondered if our classmates were now in tenth grade or something.

"It's hard to say," answered Pleskit. "Reality is a tricky concept. It's possible a few years have passed. More likely it has not been more than a few hours. It depends on how quickly the ship has been accelerating."

As I was trying to wrap my mind around this idea, and wondering how old Jordan would be when we got back (assuming, of course, that we *did* get back), the ship began to vibrate. A sudden shrieking sound seemed to split my head. My body seemed to be picking up the ship's vibrations, as if I were some giant tuning fork.

Then I felt a stretching sensation, as if I had been turned into elastic and some huge creature had grabbed my head, while some other crea-

11

ture had grabbed my feet, and now both of them were running in opposite directions.

I heard Tim screaming.

Then I realized I was doing the same thing.

"Whhhhhhhaaaaaaaaaat'sssssss   gooooooiiiiii-innnnnnggggg ooooonnnnnnnn?" I cried.

CHAPTER

3

[PLESKIT]

Trillions of Miles

I was already near *kleptra* about having been snatched away on Ellico *vec* Bur's starship. But my fear and despair doubled when I felt the undeniable stretching sensation that indicated the ship had entered an *urpelli*.

The Veeblax leaped to the floor and began changing forms so rapidly it was impossible to keep track of what it was becoming.

Urpelli jumps are very distressing for shape-shifters.

Actually, they can be distressing for anyone, so I wasn't surprised that Tim and Linnsy were

screaming in terror. After all, they had never experienced a time/space jump before. I considered screaming, too—not because of the sensation, but because of what I knew it meant: When we left the *urpelli*, we would be trillions of miles from Earth.

It is impossible to have any sense of time during a time/space jump—it is like a split second that goes on forever. (If that seems hard to understand, it's even weirder to experience!)

"What's happening to us?" cried Linnsy—

though, of course, she did not look like Linnsy at the moment, since she was so stretched out. Her words were also stretched out, which made it hard to interpret what she was saying.

"We're going through an *urpelli*," I said, my own words stretching out in the same way.

"You mean one of those holes in space you were telling us about?" she demanded.

"That's a close enough description," I said, "though it's more like a tunnel than a hole. The main thing is, we've just sidestepped the problems of lightspeed travel by stepping outside of normal spacetime. We'll drop back in soon, but I have no idea where we'll be when we do."

"So we're not about to die?" asked Tim hopefully.

Before I could answer, the jump was over, and we snapped back into our normal physical shapes.

"Nope, guess we're not about to die," said Tim, holding out his hands to study them. "Kind of a relief. For a minute there I was wondering if we were dead already."

"Dead is not the problem," said Maktel. "The problem is, since we've made a time/

15

space jump, we are now several trillion miles from Earth—which is going to make it a lot harder for us to get back."

Tim blinked. "But . . . but . . ."

"That is only part of the problem," I said. "What makes this particularly distressing is that *there is no charted urpelli* this close to Earth."

Maktel looked stunned at this news. "But an uncharted *urpelli* . . ." He let the words dangle in the air. We both knew what he was saying.

"Well, at least we have an idea of what this is all about now," I said at last, still stunned by the idea.

"You may know what's going on," said Linnsy. "I'm still totally mystified."

I glanced at Maktel. He hesitated, then nodded, a signal that he agreed I should explain to our friends what this meant. We both knew now that we had stumbled into something far bigger than we first realized. It was appropriate for Tim and Linnsy to understand as well.

"All right, here's the situation," I said. "An *urpelli* this close to Earth makes the planet enormously more valuable as a trading spot than the Trading Federation understood when they granted us the franchise. Tim, I'm sure you remember the words you found so exciting in that secret note Maktel's Motherly One wanted him to deliver to my Fatherly One."

" 'Earth is more important than you realize,' " replied Tim, quoting them instantly.

"Well, now we know why. Earth is more important than any of us had realized. In fact, the presence of this *urpelli* means your planet has the potential to become a galactic crossroads. Now I understand better why the Fatherly One has faced such opposition. Some beings obviously know about the *urpelli*, and therefore know that the trading franchise for Earth is worth far more than any of us had imagined."

Tim looked sick. "So what do you think Ellico *vec* Bur are up to?" he asked.

Before I could answer, the door of our little hiding place slid open.

CHAPTER
4
[MAKTEL]

Discovered

Ellico *vec* Bur stood in the doorway, their faces twisted with astonishment and fury.

It was not hard for Ellico *vec* Bur to have two expressions at the same time, since they were a *veccir*—a two-part being composed of separate but cooperating species. This meant, among other things, that they had two faces.

The larger face belonged to Ellico, who would have looked almost like an Earthling if not for the fact that his skin was blue and where most men would have had a beard he had writhing tentacles that (according to Tim) looked as if they had been transplanted from an octopus.

If Ellico's beard looked like it came from an octopus, the Bur part of the Trader(s) looked totally crablike, with a hard, golden-bronze shell and a small, flat face. Bur fit on Ellico's head like a cap, though I doubt you could have pried it off if you tried. The symbiont had two long legs—well, they look like legs, but they're actually called *tweezikkle*—mounted just behind its face. They extended back and down, locking themselves into Ellico's ears and forming a connection to his brain.

Ellico provided transportation and a large, active body. In exchange, Bur provided enhanced brain power and sensory ability. They claimed it was a very useful combination, but the very sight of them always made me uneasy—even when they weren't mad, which they definitely were at the moment. In fact the icy fury in both sets of eyes was so terrifying, I feared I might slip into *kleptra* right on the spot.

"What are you four doing here?" snarled the Ellico portion of the Trader(s). He did most of the talking, though he always claimed that when he did he was speaking both their thoughts. The blue tentacles of his beard were twitching with anger.

I was startled by his words. Why would the Trader(s) be surprised to find us here if they had abducted us?

"We . . . we . . . we . . ." said Pleskit, rather uselessly.

"We were looking for the Veeblax," said Linnsy. "Poor little guy got lost, and we had to hunt all over the embassy for it. I think the noise from the party scared it. I know we shouldn't have come onto your ship. But we had no idea you were going to be taking off so soon, and we were really worried about the little critter. And see," she said, gesturing toward the Veeblax, "we found it!"

"That story would make more sense if you had let us know you were here when you heard us come aboard, rather than hiding as if you were guilty of something," sneered Bur in its squeaky, scratchy voice.

"We were frightened," said Tim quickly, hauling the story back somewhat closer to the truth. "We knew we didn't belong here, even though we weren't really doing anything wrong." (Well, so much for truth. I was glad Tim wasn't connected to a fib-finder when he let loose with that *phwooper* about not doing anything wrong!) "We figured you were just coming in to pick something up and would be leaving soon—uh, leaving the ship, not the planet. Can we turn back now?"

Ellico *vec* Bur looked at him in astonishment, as if the idea that we might want to go home had not occurred to them until this moment. Bur closed its eyes, and I knew it was communicating with Ellico.

"We are not turning back," they said coldly, "so there is no point in even thinking about it. Setting aside the fact that the cost in energy would be worth more than all your lives combined, things are too . . . delicate right now for us to even consider it."

"Can you at least contact the embassy to let my Fatherly One know where we are?" asked Pleskit desperately.

"We will consider it. Doing so may be dangerous."

"How could that be?" I asked. "Won't you need to contact them to set our ransom?"

21

"Ransom?" squawked the Bur part of the Trader(s), sounding astonished.

The Ellico portion scowled. "You have thrust yourself into the middle of something that is none of your business," he said furiously. "We have no obligation to offer you any explanations."

They stepped back, and the door slid shut.

My *clinkus* tightened with guilt over the fact that I was the one who had insisted we check Ellico *vec* Bur's ship. I think it was the guilt that pushed me into saying, "Well, I guess I was right when I said those Trader(s) were up to something suspicious!"

Pleskit farted in disgust and turned his back on me.

Tim and Linnsy began to choke and cough. The Fart of Disgust is very potent.

"If you two really have to argue, could you at least wait until we've got some more open space?" gasped Linnsy.

I could not answer. I was feeling too stupid. One of the first things the Motherly One taught me after my hatching was that the worst thing to do when you have been proved right is to point that fact out.

Silence gathered and grew, even thicker and heavier in the air than Pleskit's fart. I wanted to speak, but didn't know what to say. The longer the silence lasted, the more powerful it seemed to become. So I was actually grateful to the Earthboy when he said, "Well, what are we going to do now?"

Unfortunately, the long discussion that followed turned out to be a discussion about nothing, since we didn't really have any options—other than the hope that Pleskit's Fatherly One would soon realize not only that we were missing, but that we must be on board Ellico *vec* Bur's ship.

"Even that may do us no good," said Pleskit dismally.

"Why not?" asked Tim.

"Because we went through an uncharted *urpelli*," he said patiently, and I groaned as I recognized the truth of his words.

"Which means . . . ?" prompted Linnsy.

"Which means," said Pleskit, "there's no telling where it might have spit us out. Our trail is going to be almost impossible to follow."

*   *   *

23

We slept—not easy, since there was so little space in the storage room, not to mention no soft places on which to rest. I found myself becoming agitated because I needed to *finussher.*

After considerable time had passed, the door opened and Ellico *vec* Bur slid a large metal container into our prison. The Trader(s) stepped back so quickly I wondered if they were afraid we would try to jump them or something.

"Wait!" cried Tim as the door started to slide shut. "I have to go to the bathroom!"

The door slid open again. Ellico *vec* Bur, looking exasperated, said, "All right, one at a time. You first," they added, gesturing at Tim with their walking stick.

While he was gone, I opened the metal container. "Oh, good!" I cried when I saw the gelatinous goo it held. "Food!"

"Are you *sure* that's food?" asked Linnsy, sounding uncomfortable.

"It's called *gortzwump*," said Pleskit as I reached into the container and pulled out a quivering handful of the stuff. It was orange, with green lumps. "It's a low-level food but has a solid nutritional content."

"It tastes lousy," I added. "But it will keep us alive."

"A diet of *gortzwump* keeps you alive but makes you wish you were dead," said Pleskit glumly, quoting an old Hevi-Hevian proverb.

"Nothing improves the flavor of a meal like hunger," I replied, quoting a different proverb. I began to lick the *gortzwump* off my fingers, grateful for some food at last, but secretly wishing it were something decent.

Nervously Linnsy reached into the container. "Eeeuw!" she cried. "It feels *gross!*"

"What you do not eat, I will," I replied. I was only quoting another proverb, so I was surprised when she looked offended.

Ellico *vec* Bur returned with Tim. Pleskit was the next to leave the room.

Tim declined to eat the *gortzwump*. "Wait till you get a load of the bathroom," he whispered to Linnsy. "It'll take you ten minutes just to figure out how to go!"

More time passed. We slept again. We told stories. Tim learned to eat *gortzwump*, since it became clear it was the only food we were going to get.

"Tastes like cream of wheat mixed with engine oil," he said unhappily.

We traveled through another *urpelli* and then another. *Urpelli* jumps are always disconcerting, of course. But once Tim and Linnsy got used to them they no longer found them so frightening.

I wondered where in the galaxy we might possibly be. I started to ask the question aloud but was interrupted by a sizzling sound. Suddenly the ship lurched. The movement was slight but sickening—not so much for the way it felt but for what it meant.

Lights began to flash. The wail of a siren split the air.

"Are we going through another *urpelli!*" asked Linnsy.

"That's no *urpelli!*" cried Pleskit. "We're being attacked!"

CHAPTER
5
[PLESKIT]

Space Battle

The ship lurched from side to side as Ellico *vec* Bur maneuvered to avoid the attack. The artificial gravity that had kept us on the floor now became our enemy as we flew sideways, and then upside down. The four of us tumbled against the wall, and then the ceiling. The Veeblax shrieked and sprouted wings, struggling desperately to keep itself in the air. But it was hard for it to find a safe spot with our bodies being flung back and forth, up and down, in the little room.

I saw Tim cupping his hands protectively over the *oog-slama*—which made it impossible for him to brace himself against the thudding collisions shaking all four of us. I was impressed to see him slam from floor to wall to floor, crying out in pain, but never letting go of the *oog-slama.*

Then, suddenly, our gravity disappeared. As I drifted into the center of the room, I wondered if Ellico *vec* Bur had turned off the gravity on purpose, or if the ship had automatically shut it off after a couple of such wild swings. Or—more frightening—had the gravity mechanism been damaged by the attack? Was it possible we were now a "wounded bird"—a ship with no way to navigate or propel itself, doomed to drift through space forever?

Who was attacking us anyway? And why? Were we near a planet? Surely none of the civilized worlds would attack a ship this way.

For a moment I wondered if the attack came from someone trying to *rescue* us. But when the little vessel trembled and shook under another direct hit, I realized that this would be an extremely bad way to go about a rescue. I was keenly aware that only a thin metal shell separated us from the incredible void of space, from the frozen vacuum that would end our lives immediately should the hull be breached.

Suddenly Ellico *vec* Bur's voices came through the speaker. "Stowaways! Get up here and into some seats!"

At the same time the door of our little room slid open.

Clutching the Veeblax, which was squealing with terror, I led the way to the passenger cabin. It wasn't easy to move with the gravity off, of course, and we had to bounce from wall to wall. It was even harder for Tim and Linnsy, who had no practice in zero gravity. Finally Maktel and I grabbed their arms to pull them along with us. This was easy enough to do, of course, since neither of them weighed anything.

From our exploration of the ship (before Ellico *vec* Bur's unexpected arrival caused us to scramble for a hiding place) I knew that the largest passenger cabin—located just behind and separate from the pilot's room—had six padded seats.

When we reached the cabin, I could see Ellico *vec* Bur through the door that led to the pilot's area. The Trader(s) were totally focused on their piloting duties. But they must have heard us come in because, without turning their heads from the console, they snapped, "Strap your-selves in. Now! *MOVE!*"

Another explosion shook the ship.

"Who's attacking us?" asked Tim.

Ellico *vec* Bur ignored him.

The ship was shuddering, clearly badly dam-aged now. We floated above the vibrating floor. Linnsy grabbed the arm of one of the chairs, then pulled herself into the seat. She started to say, "Where are the seat bel—" but before she could finish the sentence, the safety belts had wrapped themselves around her.

Ignoring her startled squawk, I pulled myself into a seat, too. I felt a little safer once the straps and pads had positioned themselves around me. The Veeblax snuggled in beside me, whimpering in terror. I glanced around and was relieved to see that Tim and Maktel had man-aged to get themselves secured as well.

"All right, listen," snarled Ellico *vec* Bur. "We had almost finished our trip; the planet I was heading for is right below us. So we're

going to try to land. We've got no choice, actually. But it's not going to be pleasant. Get ready
for a rough ride."

I thought it had already been a rough ride, but
a moment later we hit the atmosphere and the
Trader(s)' warning suddenly made sense.

It's amazing that air can be so solid. But if
you think of the difference in the way water
feels when you slip your hand gently in and
when you slap it, then you can understand
why striking air at our speed was so bone
shaking.

Ellico *vec* Bur cursed as we bounced off the
atmosphere. We made two more skips, like a
stone across the surface of a pond. Then, suddenly, we pierced the planet's airshell and were
hurtling for the surface.

The ship was badly wounded—I could tell
from the various smells that several different
things were burning—and it twisted and
lurched wildly as we seared our way through
the sky. I am not ashamed to admit that all four
of us passengers were squealing with terror.

Whatever else I might think of Ellico *vec* Bur,
I had to admit that their piloting was masterful.

The Trader(s)'s skill at the control panel saved all our lives.

Through the viewscreen I could see that we were hurtling toward an area of lush jungle.

"Brace yourselves!" shouted the Trader(s). "We're about to—"

And then we hit. Despite the piloting skills of Ellico *vec* Bur, despite our protective seats, the impact when we struck the surface knocked us all senseless. The last I remember was a horrendous screeching sound, a burst of light, and a smell of smoke.

Then blackness surrounded me.

CHAPTER

6

[L I N N S Y]

Wounded

I seemed to be swimming through a sea of darkness. My body felt as if I had been put through a washing machine with a load of stones. Strange smells filled me with a sense of approaching doom.

Suddenly I gasped and opened my eyes.

"Mom?" I cried. "Dad? Where are you?"

Then I saw the weird colors and strange decorations above me, and it all came back to me: I was in Ellico *vec* Bur's ship, and we had just crashed on a planet trillions of miles from Earth.

The smell of smoke drove away my concerns about my pain. We had to get out of here!

Or had the others already gone?

"Tim?" I whispered.

No answer.

"Tim?" I said again, more loudly. "Pleskit? Maktel? *Anyone?*"

No answer.

I started to shake. What if I was the only one who had lived through the crash? I would be stranded, alone, in a jungle on a strange world trillions of miles from Earth. Did this planet even have breathable air? And how would I know if it did?

I had never felt so alone in my life.

I stretched my neck to look around. Tim was in the seat next to me. His eyes were closed, and I couldn't see enough of him to tell if he was breathing. A cold fear seized me. Was he unconscious . . . or dead?

I tried to stand, but the seat's straps and pads held me tight. I struggled against the restraints, but they only held me tighter. "Stupid seat!" I screamed, terrified that the automatic release was broken and that I would be trapped in a burning ship. Then I realized that I was the one being stupid, letting panic get in the way of clear thought. I began running my hands over the arms, looking for a release mechanism. Finally I found the right button, and the pads and straps slid swiftly and silently away. I jumped to my feet in relief.

"Thanks, seat," I said, my anger at being trapped dissolved in the realization that the seat had probably saved my life. I gave it a grateful pat, then picked my way across the crumpled floor to Tim.

I never thought I would be so happy to see that kid breathing.

I shook him.

"Not now, Mom," he muttered. "It's Saturday."

"Tim," I whispered urgently. "Tim, wake up!"

He groaned. Then his eyelids fluttered open. He gasped and tried to leap to his feet, but the restraints held him in place, just as they had done to me. "Where are we?" he cried.

"Shhhh! We're still in Ellico *vec* Bur's ship. It crashed. We're the first ones awake." I hesitated, then added softly, "Actually, we may be the only ones alive. I haven't had a chance to check on the others."

I showed Tim where to press the button to get the seat to release him. It didn't work.

"Linnsy!" he cried. "You've got to get me out of here!"

"I'll find something to cut it open," I said. "But first I have to check on Pleskit and Maktel."

The smoky smell was getting stronger. Even though I couldn't see open flames I wondered if the ship was going to explode—and, if so, how much time we had to get out of it.

Then two more questions hit me: Would we be able to use the door, or had it been damaged in the crash? And if it did work, would we be able to breathe the air of this planet?

I pushed those fears aside. *One problem at a time*, I told myself firmly. I didn't have time, then, to be amazed at how calm I was able to stay, at how strong and clear I felt.

Pleskit was just starting to stir. Maktel was breathing but still out cold. I decided to let them come out of it on their own while I tried to free Tim. But before I had a chance to work on his seat, I heard a cry of despair from the pilot's cabin and realized that I should check on Ellico *vec* Bur, too.

How did I end up in this mess? I wondered as I hurried forward. *I'm just a kid. I don't belong on another planet!*

The Trader(s) were slumped sideways in their seat. I stood next to them for a moment, uncertain of what to do. I reached forward, then drew my hand back, frightened. Had that cry been the sound of one of them dying?

I wondered if I should check for a heartbeat—or maybe two heartbeats. But even if Bur had a heart, I doubted I could feel it beat through the hard shell of its body.

The tentacles of Ellico's beard began to twitch. I jumped back, surprised and a little disgusted. Even so, it seemed like a good sign.

I moved forward again. As I did, Bur opened its golden eyes.

"What are you doing?" it asked.

The scratchy sound of the creature's voice made me shiver.

"I . . . I was checking to see if you were all right."

"We are not. My partner is hurt, though I cannot tell how badly. You must free us from the constraints of this seat."

I hesitated. What I *wanted* to do was get as far away from this weird and scary duo as I could. But I reminded myself that their piloting had probably just saved our lives.

I reached for the release mechanism under the arm of the seat.

Nothing happened.

"It's jammed," said Bur. "You'll have to cut us free."

I heard a groan from the passenger cabin and glanced back. Maktel was stirring. "Just a minute," I said. "I have to check on one of the others."

"Come back!" screeched Bur.

Ignoring it, I hurried into the passenger cabin.

Tim was still struggling to get out of his seat. Maktel's release button must have worked because he was on his feet. He was leaning against the seatback, one hand pressed to his head, obviously still unsteady. Pleskit remained in his seat. He looked dazed, but at least his eyes were wide open.

"I'm all right," he said, when he saw me looking at him. "I just need a minute."

"Linnsy!" shrieked Bur. "Get back here!"

Maktel looked up. "Ignore them!" he said, his voice low but intense. "We've got to get out of here."

"We can't just leave them," I said, shocked at the idea.

"They're dangerous!"

"Get in here and help us!" Bur's high scratchy voice, which was incredibly annoying to listen to, sounded frantic.

Ignoring Maktel's angry shouts, I scurried back to the pilot's cabin.

The smoke was getting thicker.

"Open that little door," said Bur. "The one down there. No, over there!"

For the first time I realized the helplessness of the little creature. Locked onto Ellico's head, it could not move or even make a gesture on its own.

It took a few tries for me to find the door it meant. Bur's impatient squawkings as I searched began to upset me. Even worse was the smoke; it was thick and vile-smelling, and was making me cough.

Finally I located the door and popped it open. Inside I found a toolbox—and inside the toolbox a silvery blade.

"Cut us free!" demanded Bur.

I did as it asked. But the Ellico portion of the symbiote remained unconscious, so they still couldn't move.

"Is Ellico going to be all right?" I asked.

"I don't know," said Bur, and the fear and concern I heard so plainly in its voice were unexpectedly touching.

"Linnsy!" cried Maktel. "Come on!"

"We can't leave Ellico *vec* Bur here!" I replied.

Then I remembered that Tim was still trapped in his seat. I scurried back to the passenger cabin and used the silver blade to cut him free.

"Come on!" I said as he staggered to his feet. "Help me!"

I ran back to the pilot's cabin. A moment later Tim and Pleskit came stumbling in, the Veeblax close at their heels.

With the boys' help, I hauled the Trader(s) to their feet. It took all three of us to get them through the door into the passenger cabin. It was slow work, and tense, because the smoke was billowing out behind us now, and I was terrified that the ship was going to explode at any minute.

"Come on!" cried Maktel, dancing urgently from one foot to the other. "We've got to get out of here!"

CHAPTER
7
[MAKTEL]

Stranded

Much as I feared Ellico *vec* Bur, I did understand that we had a moral duty to remove the Trader(s) from the ship. So while Tim and Pleskit went to help Linnsy haul the *veccir* from their seat, I searched for the mechanism to open the outer door. I checked the atmo-reader before opening it, of course. Assuming the device had not been damaged by the crash, the air outside was a little rich in oxygen and had more nitrogen than I really liked, but was clearly safe for us to breathe.

I pulled the handle.

The door swung down, revealing a dense jungle. The ship was resting in a cloud of fireproof lavender foam, so at least our external safety systems were working. It was a good thing, too. Otherwise we might have found ourselves in the middle of a raging forest fire.

I hoped the internal safety systems were also working. The inward rush of oxygen-rich air—warm, damp, and sweet—would encourage any fires that might be on the verge of breaking out. It was hard to tell whether the smoke meant the safety systems had successfully *quenched* any potential fires, or that the ship was in danger of bursting into flames at any moment.

I wanted to bolt and run. Then Pleskit, Linnsy, and Tim came back into the passenger cabin, dragging Ellico *vec* Bur's limp body with them.

"Maktel, come here and help!" ordered Linnsy, who could be quite bossy.

I went to her side and took one of the Trader(s)'s feet. With Tim and Pleskit holding the Trader(s)'s shoulders, we picked them up and carried them down the door—which also acted as a ramp.

"Another planet," said Tim as we reached the

ground. His voice was filled with wonder. "We're standing on *another planet!*"

"Well, we'd better stand a little farther from the ship if we're going to *survive* on this planet," I said sharply. "Let's keep moving, just in case it decides to explode."

It wasn't easy to get away from the ship. Not only were we still carrying Ellico *vec* Bur, but the underbrush was thick and clinging, and kept tripping us.

"I hope none of this stuff is poisonous," muttered Pleskit.

It was a reasonable fear. Even a brief study of the plant life of the galaxy can leave one in awe of the strange and terrible ways plants have of protecting themselves—as our Earthling friends learned when we finally came to a clear space far enough from the ship that we felt it was safe to stop and put Ellico *vec* Bur down.

I bent over and put my hands on my knees, exhausted from the effort. I heard Linnsy walk away.

Next thing I knew, she was screaming.

Looking up, I saw that she had been attacked by a strange vine. Its thick tendrils had wrapped themselves around her legs. Weird orange pods were creeping toward her, making a sucking sound as they approached.

Linnsy struck at them. They flinched, drawing back some two or three feet. But at the same time one of them spit a wad of steaming purple fluid that just missed her face.

Before I could think of what to do, I heard a cry of rage from Tim. He ran toward the vine, brandishing a piece of metal. I realized he must have wrenched it from the wreckage of the ship.

"Stop it!" he screamed, hacking at the vine. "Stop it! Stop it! *Stop it!*"

Gouts of purple fluid burst out wherever he struck the vine. It writhed as he hacked at it, and the orange pods were squealing as they backed away, a horrible, high-pitched scream that was like needles in my ears. Three of the pods spit clots of the steaming purple fluid. Two missed, but one struck Tim's arm. He screamed in agony but seemed to gain strength from his pain. Slashing and hacking, he attacked the vine with new fury.

Suddenly the thick tendrils unwrapped them-

selves from Linnsy's feet and slid into the ground, disappearing so rapidly it was as if they had never been there.

Tim staggered over to Linnsy, clutching his arm where the plantspit had hit it. "You okay?" he asked grimly.

"Yeah," she said, though she was trembling. "And you?"

"Not sure. I never did anything like that before. Man, this *hurts!*"

As he said this, he moved his hand. Pleskit and I moved in closer to get a look. The plantspit had seared a long mark across his arm—a mark that was already beginning to blister.

"I don't like the look of that," said Pleskit. Then he took Tim's hand and said, "That was well done. I am ashamed I did not help. The truth is, Earthlings are much more geared to action than we are. Our studies indicate that this is the source of many of your problems. But it certainly comes in useful in a situation like this!"

"You're not kidding," said Linnsy, who was still shaking. "I thought I was done for. Thanks, pal."

"I think it was all those episodes of *Tarbox Moon Warriors* I've watched kicking in," said Tim shyly.

I heard a noise behind me. Turning, I saw that Ellico *vec* Bur had gotten to their feet. Cursing, one arm tucked close to their side, they staggered back toward the ship.

"What are they doing?" asked Pleskit in concern as they climbed the ramp. "Aren't they afraid it's going to blow up?"

"Who cares?" I said. "This is our chance to get away from them!"

"Why should we do that?" asked Linnsy. "They're the only ones who might know where we are!"

"They're also dangerous villains! Who knows what they might do to us next? We pulled them out of the ship, got them to safety. If they want to go back in, that's their problem!"

"We don't really know that they're villains," said Tim. "From the way they reacted when they found out we were on board, it doesn't seem like they took off with us on purpose."

"All right," I said angrily. "You stay here and be nice. I'm leaving!"

"Where are you going?" asked Pleskit.

"I saw a city on the way down. We should head for that. We'll probably be able to find an embassy there. If we do, they'll contact your Fatherly One for us."

"Do you have any idea how to get there?" asked Linnsy, with more skepticism than I thought was justified.

"As a matter of fact, I do," I replied, trying not to sound as smug as I felt. "It was ahead of us as we were coming down. So was the sun. Therefore, if we walk toward the sun, we will be walking toward the city!"

"We'll have to go through the jungle," said Tim nervously.

"Would you prefer to stay here with Ellico *vec* Bur?" I asked.

Tim looked confused.

"I think we should go with Maktel," said Pleskit, which annoyed me a little, since he wasn't really saying he thought I was right, just that we should stick together.

Though they sounded reluctant, Tim and Linnsy agreed. So we aimed ourselves at the sun, which was blue, and began walking.

"This is so cool," said Tim as we made our way among the trees. They were as thick across as I am tall, and soared so high we couldn't see their tops. "It's just the kind of place I always dreamed of visiting when I was watching *Tarbox Moon Warriors*," he continued. "Man, look at those flowers! At least, I think they're flowers. . . ."

The things he was pointing to were a blazing red and as large as my head. They were lovely, and their scent was compelling. But given our first experience with the flora of this planet, I was not interested in picking one. I was afraid it might try to eat my face or something.

In fact, we were all terrified of encountering another of the vicious vines. So we moved with extreme caution.

We had been walking for about a *kerbleck* when something began buzzing around my head.

"These are the weirdest insects I ever saw," complained Linnsy. I saw that she was surrounded by a cloud of the same creatures, which were about the size of my thumb.

"Actually, I don't think they're insects," said

Tim. "How can an insect have fur? They're more like hairy hummingbirds."

"You cannot expect to find exactly the same kind of animal classifications here that you did on Earth," I said impatiently.

Pushing aside a wall of feathery stems, I stepped forward, bumped into something, and started to scream.

CHAPTER
8
[TIM]

Eargon Fooz

I wasn't sure about Maktel's idea that we should get away from Ellico *vec* Bur and head for the city, but I was so distracted by the pain in my arm where the plant had spit on me that I couldn't think of anything better to suggest. The spot that had been burned by the plantspit had never stopped hurting. Now, as we stumbled through the jungle, constantly checking the sun (when we could see it) to be sure we were heading in the right direction, it began to throb worse than ever.

Then the "hairy hummingbirds" began buzzing around us. When I raised my arm to swat them away I saw green streaks stretching across my skin, radiating out from the spot where the plant had burned me.

I felt a sickening lurch in my stomach. Was this some weird alien infection?

Was I going to turn into a plant?

Before I could say anything, Maktel began to scream.

Looking up, I squawked myself.

Rising directly ahead of us was a yellow wall of fernlike plants, about eight feet high. Maktel had pushed aside some of the plants to step through, an action that had brought him face to face with a creature that had been coming from the other direction.

Well, not quite face to face. It was more like face to belly, since the creature was quite a bit taller than Maktel. It had four legs, which wouldn't have been that unusual (from an Earthling point of view) except that it also had two arms, with well-developed hands attached.

The creature's skin was slick and smooth, almost like vinyl. I can't tell you what color it was, since it had a lot of colors. Not only that, the colors tended to move and shift.

"It's camouflaging itself," whispered Linnsy in awe.

"You're right!" I replied, watching in fascination. The creature was changing color the way a chameleon does, except that these color changes were far faster and vastly more complex, picking up the look of the jungle around us in great detail—the purple tree bark, the bright green leaves with their thick yellow veins, the brown and purple pods that hung from the trees, and the way the light coming through the trees made shades and shadows from all of that.

The creature's hindquarters looked like those of a small horse. In front the arms came out at about shoulder level. They were attached to a long neck—about half again as long as a horse of the same size would have had. At the end of the neck was a strange and beautiful face. Again, the face was somewhat horselike, but broader, so that there was room for all four eyes—two that looked straight ahead, two that watched to the sides. Four pointed ears moved constantly, as if checking in all directions.

We had clearly startled the creature as much

as it had startled us, for it stumbled back, putting a hand to its mouth and making a little cry of alarm.

Pleskit immediately spread his arms and held his hands open. Maktel, once he stopped screaming, repeated the gesture. It took me a moment to realize that this was a way of indicating that they had no weapons and meant no harm. I imitated the gesture. At a little nudge from my outstretched right hand, so did Linnsy.

"*Ikbu!*" said Pleskit quietly.

"*Ikbu,*" responded the creature.

I glanced down, and was amused to see that the Veeblax was working on doing an imitation of the creature. It wasn't bad for a first try.

Pleskit began to babble at our new acquaintance in a language I had never heard him use before. (I had heard enough Hevi-Hevian to realize this was not it.)

The creature babbled back. After a moment Pleskit turned to me and Linnsy and said, "Her name is Eargon Fooz, and she is willing to help us on our journey."

"I don't know," said Maktel darkly. "Do you think we should trust her?"

I was sick of him being so suspicious. I could tell Pleskit and Linnsy were, too.

Only I was the one who said it out loud.

"I will be glad to step blindly into this potential trap if you will give me one reason we should trust this being," Maktel replied sharply.

I didn't have any, of course; the best I could come up with was "Give me one reason we should *distrust* her."

Pleskit said, "According to *Wakkam* Akkim, many choices in life are finally decided by whether you think the universe is basically good or basically out to get you."

"According to the Motherly One," responded Maktel, "blind trust is the mark of a fool."

Eargon Fooz was watching this conversation in puzzlement.

As it worked out, I was the one who settled the matter. I did not do this by making a brilliant point. I did it by putting out my hand to get Pleskit's attention, which caused Linnsy to shout, "Tim, look at your arm!"

I did, and nearly fainted. The green streaks were starting to rise up like the veins on my grandmother's legs.

Eargon Fooz made an alarming noise, then ran off a string of words I can't begin to repeat.

Pleskit looked alarmed. "She says your arm needs to be treated immediately. We have to go to her village."

"How do we know she's not just making that up?" demanded Maktel. "Who knows what might happen if we go to her village? We don't even know if she represents the civilized species on this planet. We might be attacked, beaten, robbed, served for dinner—"

"Oh, stop!" said Pleskit sharply.

I was feeling lightheaded with fear at what was happening to me, but not so light-headed that I didn't have time to also feel annoyed at Maktel for making things so much more frightening.

Then I wondered if he was right to be suspicious, and I was the stupid one for being so trusting.

Eargon Fooz turned to face him, speaking to him again in that strange language.

Maktel began to back away, babbling something I could not understand.

He was still babbling when Eargon Fooz leaped forward and snatched him off the ground.

CHAPTER
9
[PLESKIT]

Jungle Journey

"Let me go!" shouted Maktel. "LET ME GO!"

Eargon Fooz had Maktel's arms pinned to his sides, but my friend was flailing his legs wildly, and landed a couple of solid kicks against her chest. As he did, a vine shot out of the ground, reaching for his foot. Eargon Fooz spun him away, and it missed.

Maktel stopped kicking and stared at the vine in horror.

"The plant you were backing toward is very dangerous," said Eargon Fooz quietly as she set Maktel gently to the ground a safe distance from the killer vine. "It would have melted off your feet if it had caught you."

Maktel can be very suspicious. But he is also gracious, which is one of the things I like about him. Crossing his hands over his chest, he bowed his head and said humbly, "I am in your service."

"Service is not required," said Eargon Fooz. "However, a little less noise would be appreciated.

"What are they saying?" asked Tim, who was standing next to me.

I translated, realizing I was going to be doing a lot of that as long as we were with Eargon Fooz—or anywhere on this planet, for that matter.

"How come you speak her language?" asked Linnsy.

"Well, it's not really *her* language," I said. "We've been speaking in Standard Galactic."

Linnsy looked puzzled. "Is that different from Hevi-Hevian?"

"Yes. Most planets have their own language. But everyone who is part of the Unified Galaxy also learns Standard Galactic from the time *yeeble* is little. After all, it's very hard to have a unified civilization when you are splintered by separate languages."

"Let us begin our journey," said Eargon Fooz. "We can talk as we travel. I do not want to delay getting treatment for your friend."

I translated most of this for Linnsy and Tim, leaving out the last part for fear of alarming Tim unnecessarily. We started out. The Veeblax rode on my shoulder, and I was so concerned about the vicious plants that I considered trying to figure out some way to bind my pet to me so it would not scamper off on an exploration and get eaten. But for reasons that should be obvious, it is hard to tie down a shapeshifter.

I noticed Tim continually cupping his hand over the *oog-slama* and hoped, for both their sakes, that this adventure would not prevent the thing from maturing.

Our path led us through amazing and beautiful territory. We walked, for a time, along the edge of a cliff, with a sheer drop of hundreds of feet to our right. This gave us a clear view of the city that was our goal. Its spires and towers reared high in the lavender sky. The clear, unpolluted air above it indicated that the people were civilized, and I began to feel that Maktel had been right to insist we head for it. If we could make it there safely, we could get medical treatment for Tim's arm. Once that was taken care of, we could almost certainly find an embassy where my diplomatic identification would be recognized. Then our problems would be over.

As we traveled, Eargon Fooz told me that the planet we were on was called Billa Kindikan, at least by her people. "It means 'beautiful world,'" she said proudly.

She didn't want to talk much about her tribe; I got the feeling her people weren't crazy about off-worlders. I wondered if they had had a bad experience with Traders.

"Is the planet part of the Federation?" I asked.

"We have been invited to join, but have chosen not to," she replied.

After a while the path led back into deep jungle. The smells here were so rich and varied they almost made me dizzy. Brightly colored birds—or, at least, creatures with wings—flitted among the branches. Distant growls made us nervous, though Eargon Fooz laughed and told us not to worry about them.

"Easy for her to say," muttered Maktel.

Though we saw some flowers, most of the plants had pods instead—some round, some cone shaped, some bursting with spikes. They were mostly shades of yellow, sometimes blending toward green, sometimes toward brown, sometimes with a streak or cap of purple. Given what we had already been through, the sight of so many pods made us all nervous, wondering which of them might be fatally dangerous.

"Do not worry," said Eargon Fooz, when she realized our concern. "My people keep the paths clear of the killer plants. As long as you stay with me, you will be safe."

I wanted to ask Maktel how far he thought we would have gotten without Eargon Fooz's guidance, but decided against it. We didn't need any more tension right now. Besides, he would probably claim she was making those comments about the path just to lull us into a false sense of security.

"Listen!" said Linnsy suddenly. "What's that?"

"Waterfall," replied Eargon Fooz, once I had translated the question.

She should have said *big* waterfall, since when we finally saw it, far off to our left, we realized that it was several hundred feet high.

"It's beautiful!" cried Linnsy. "Can we go closer?"

"That would be pleasant," said Eargon Fooz, "but probably not wise under the circumstances. Right now it is important that we keep moving."

Though she didn't say it out loud, I knew our guide was concerned about Tim. I glanced at him, feeling a little guilty that I had not been paying closer attention to him. The green, veiny things on his arm were thicker, and getting brighter. His face, in contrast, was getting pale. He looked as if he were in pain.

"I'm all right," he said, when I asked him about it. But a few minutes later, when Eargon Fooz offered him a ride, he took it gratefully.

I was more glad than ever that she was with us when we reached the place where we had to cross the river. It was wild and white with froth as it smashed and splashed around enormous boulders. It was also about forty feet below us, since it traveled through a channel it had carved out over the centuries. It would have been nice if there had been a bridge across this chasm, which was some fifty feet across.

Alas, there was not—unless you're willing to count a single log no wider than my head as a bridge.

"You've got to be kidding!" said Maktel, when he realized our guide expected us to cross on this.

Eargon Fooz, clearly not willing to take his fearful reaction as speaking for the entire group, looked at Linnsy and me. Tim was still on her back; I could tell she was planning on carrying him across no matter what the rest of us decided.

"Such a crossing is not something we can do with ease or confidence," I said apologetically.

"All right, then I will have to carry all of you," she replied. "Wait here while I take your friend across."

Eargon Fooz was a large being, her own body much wider than the log, and I was terrified for

both her and Tim when I saw her leap up onto it. But she moved with a delicate grace and was soon standing on the far side.

"Are you sure you don't want to cross on your own?" she called back.

I looked at the bridge, then down at the smashing, roaring water. I knew that if I had no other choice, I would be willing to attempt the crossing. I also knew that, since I *did* have a choice, I would be insane to try it on my own.

"Please come and get us!" I called.

Tim crawled off her back, and she recrossed the bridge quickly and deftly. One by one she carried us across. I was the last to go, and I kept my eyes closed for about half the trip. I only opened them when I heard the others start to scream.

"Hold on!" ordered Eargon Fooz. She began to run. I flung my arms around her neck and held on as if I was trying to become a *vec* with her. The Veeblax clutched my own neck with equal fervor.

Eargon Fooz's sudden burst of speed caused the log to shift beneath us. I cried out in alarm, but Eargon Fooz was nimble, and the shifting bridge didn't seem to bother her at all.

Or maybe she simply didn't fear death.

I was feeling enough fear for both of us, terrified by both the sight of the raging water that swept along below us as we sped over the bridge and the frantic cries of my friends.

CHAPTER
10
[TIM]

It's Not Easy Turning Green

After Eargon Fooz had put me down and gone back for the others, I sat and stared at my arm. I felt sick with fear—not the stomach lurching fear you feel when some sudden horrible thing happens, but the slow fear that comes when you sense lurking doom.

I was so involved in wondering if I was turning into a plant that I scarcely looked up when Eargon Fooz came back with Linnsy. But when she dropped off Maktel, he interrupted my thoughts by sitting down next to me and saying, "How are you feeling, Tim?"

He sounded really concerned. Trying not to

show how much this surprised me, I said, "A little woozy, I guess, but not bad other than that. Except—" I stopped, then decided to take a chance. "Except I'm scared."

"I would be, too," said Maktel quietly. "Well, actually, I *am* scared. But I'd be even more scared if . . ." He glanced down at my arm but didn't say anything else.

I looked at him in surprise. Maybe he wasn't a complete creep after all. I didn't have time to think about that, because suddenly I felt a set of tiny claws digging into my neck. Springing to my feet, I heard a screech—and then cries of horror from Linnsy and Maktel.

Each of them was fighting off five or six little creatures that had swarmed onto them. The creatures, about the size of my hand, were covered with orange-yellow fur. They had enormous eyes and would have been very cute if not for their pointed, pushed-up noses. Well, that and their needle-sharp claws and teeth.

Suddenly the creature that had jumped onto my neck made a sound that I can only think indicated disgust. It leaped away and landed on Linnsy, who was desperately trying to swat away the ones already climbing over her. The little beasts clung to her, squealing in outrage, as if they were astonished she would dare try to get rid of them.

I had been feeling weak and sick, but the sight of my friends being attacked brought on a surge of energy.

"You let go of her!" I cried as I grabbed one of the creatures attacking Linnsy. I wrenched it away. I was terrified by its snapping teeth and wondered if I would catch yet another alien disease if it bit me. But I couldn't let it get Linnsy.

At first the thing struggled to get away from me. Then, suddenly, it went limp. I hurled the wretched thing into the bushes and snatched two more from Linnsy's legs. They reacted the same way the first one had, struggling, then falling still. I flung them away but was horrified to see still more of the little monsters leaping out from the trees.

Maktel was batting at the ones on his legs, shrieking for help. I pulled two away from him. Same reaction.

Then another two *dozen* of the little beasts reached us. They leaped for Maktel and Linnsy, who stumbled and fell to the ground. I threw myself down and began plucking the monsters away, without time to wonder why I seemed to be immune to them.

Suddenly Eargon Fooz came galloping up. Pleskit was clinging to her back, looking terrified.

Eargon Fooz threw back her head and made a sound unlike any I had ever heard—a high-pitched squeal that seemed to slice right through my head.

The creatures stopped as if frozen.

Eargon Fooz repeated the horrible sound.

The creatures scrambled off Linnsy and Maktel and began to back away, crawling slowly, never taking their eyes off Eargon Fooz.

"*Krimlikzl,*" she said in disgust. I wondered if that was what the creatures were called, or if it was some swear word on this planet.

I began examining the pouch that held the *oog-slama,* suddenly terrified that the Veeblax-to-be might have been damaged in the fight.

Eargon Fooz continued to speak.

Pleskit translated:

"She says that the creatures are called *krim-likzl.* They are stupid and dangerous, and all the more dangerous because they are stupid. They are actually a tribe. They have a truce with Eargon Fooz's people and are not supposed to attack them, or anyone under their protection."

"What were they after?" asked Linnsy nervously. "Were they going to eat us?"

Pleskit translated the question for Eargon Fooz, listened to her answer, then said, "They were going to feed us to their babies. That's why they didn't bite you. They were saving you for later."

"That's gross!" cried Linnsy.

"Why didn't they attack Tim?" asked Maktel. "They seemed almost afraid of him."

Eargon Fooz hesitated. When she finally spoke, her answer filled me with fear, and a sense of doom.

"There is something in his body they do not like."

What was this plant poison doing to me?

Though I had wanted to travel to other planets for as long as I can remember, wanted it so much that it kept me awake some nights, so much I could feel it almost like an ache, that desire was nothing compared to how much I now longed to be back home, to see my mother, to let her take care of me.

To feel safe again.

What I did feel, suddenly, was exhausted, as if the battle had used up my entire supply of energy for the day. I groaned and felt myself begin to sway.

"Help him onto my back," said Eargon Fooz.

I felt myself boosted up. I wrapped my arms around her long neck and leaned forward, trying to stay alert enough not to fall off as she moved into the jungle again.

Though none of them said anything, I noticed that Linnsy, Pleskit, and even Maktel were careful to make sure that at least one of them was never more than a few feet away from me.

At first this was a little annoying. But as the day went on, and I felt worse and worse, I began to appreciate their concern.

Several hours later, as the sky was beginning to grow dark, we came to Eargon Fooz's village. It consisted of about thirty or forty circular houses, each about forty feet across and topped by a thick roof of leaves.

When we reached the edge of the village, a group of five creatures that looked like small versions of Eargon Fooz burst out of one of the houses and galloped over to surround us. They began chattering excitedly in what seemed to be yet another language. Eargon Fooz laughed and embraced them one by one, kissing each on his or her forehead.

"That's so sweet," whispered Linnsy, who was standing close beside me. (I was still clinging to Eargon Fooz's back, of course.)

After a few minutes Eargon Fooz turned and said something to Pleskit, speaking in Standard Galactic.

"They are her children," he translated—which was pretty much what I had figured.

Other villagers came out to greet Eargon Fooz, and to learn about us strangers. She answered a few questions—at least, I assume that was what she was doing—then pressed through the crowd.

"She wants us to meet her Significant Elders," explained Pleskit.

These turned out to be the five oldest members of the tribe. They were gathered in the

largest of the circular buildings, which was decorated inside with beautiful weavings made
from vines and stems.

They looked startled when Eargon Fooz
brought us in to see them, but they listened carefully as she told them our story. Then she pushed
me forward so they could look at my arm.

They studied it carefully, shaking their heads
in a way I didn't like. After murmuring among
themselves for a while, they spoke to Eargon
Fooz, who translated what they said into
Standard Galactic for Pleskit and Maktel, who
then translated it again for Linnsy and me.

"They say you must go to the Worms of
Wisdom," said Pleskit.

"What are they?" I asked nervously.

Pleskit translated my question for the Elders.
Their answer was not entirely satisfactory:
"You'll see when you get there."

We couldn't leave until morning, so that
night the villagers had a feast in our honor. I
would say that it was a vegetarian feast, but
even though it seemed as if everything we ate
came from plants, on this world the dividing

line between plants and animals seemed pretty iffy. Some of the stuff smelled so bad I couldn't even try it. I noticed this did not stop Maktel, who ate a little of everything.

"Look at Maktel," whispered Pleskit.

"Yeah, I know," I said, thinking Pleskit was embarrassed because our companion was being such a pig. I'm glad I didn't say that, because Pleskit's next words were, "I wish I could eat that way."

"Why?" I asked in suprise.

Pleskit seemed startled by the question. "Well, it is a very important skill for a diplomat. Sharing food is probably the most basic way that peoples connect everywhere in the galaxy. Therefore, the more foods you can bring yourself to eat, the better the chance you have of making a positive impression. Besides, a wide range of eating habits makes travel infinitely more pleasurable."

If I hadn't been feeling so sick, I might have taken that as a challenge. As it was, I let Pleskit direct me toward things he thought I would like. With his help Linnsy and I were able to eat about a third of the foods they served, including a thick stew that tasted of roast pork and was about as good as anything I've ever had.

After the feast we returned to Eargon Fooz's house to sleep. Her children were romping around, wrestling and snorting, which was something that she seemed to enjoy watching.

"They have good energy," she said contentedly. Then she called them together so that Pleskit could show them the Veeblax's shapeshifting tricks, which made them all laugh. Then she gave each of them a light spank on the rump and told them it was time for bed—which, basically, meant finding on the floor a place that you liked.

After Eargon Fooz finally got her younglings settled down, she invited me to come and cuddle in between her and her littlest one, who was named Sidron Fuzzle.

I was glad to accept. I felt cold and sick, and I was very frightened by the way the green things on my arm were still growing.

What I really wanted was my mother.

Eargon Fooz was the closest thing I was going to find on this planet.

CHAPTER
11
[TIM]

The Wisdom of the Worms

The Worms of Wisdom lived in a cave at the base of a steep mountain. The cliffs that towered above the cave mouth were reddish-orange and seemed to sparkle in the afternoon sun. Though I tried to walk, I was exhausted within half an hour after we started out, and rode most of the way on Eargon Fooz's back.

Linnsy walked close beside us, watching me carefully.

To reach the worms we had to go deep underground, traveling through chilly chambers of stone that were connected by narrow tunnels like a series of beads on a string. The chambers would have been pitch black had not Eargon Fooz given each of my companions a small lantern with a wick that burned some sort of plant oil. I found myself hoping that the oil came from the same plants that had attacked us, hoping that Eargon Fooz's people gathered those rotten pods and squashed them horribly to extract the oil.

After an hour or so we came to a mist-filled cavern. It was lit by thousands of dimly glowing, apple-sized spheres that drifted slowly through the mist, floating between five and ten feet above the bubbling lake that covered most of the cavern floor. Jagged towers of stone thrust up from dark water, rising so high they were lost to sight.

Eargon Fooz slapped her hand against the wall and let out a cry that echoed through the cavern.

The water bubbled and churned. Suddenly thousands of tiny heads burst through the surface of the water, not more than four feet from where we stood. All four of us off-worlders cried out in surprise and stumbled backward.

"Alla imkim dibble kidit, Eargon Fooz?"

asked the heads. They spoke in perfect unison, and though each voice was tiny, together they seemed to fill the stony space.

Eargon Fooz turned her long neck and said, "They ask why I disturb their rest." (She said this in Standard Galactic, of course, and Pleskit translated it for Linnsy and me. From here on in, I'll just give the translations.)

"We come seeking wisdom," Eargon Fooz told the worms. "Also, to ask if you can heal the off-worlder who is turning green."

"Let us see him," said the worms.

Eargon Fooz took my arm, and I staggered forward, sick with fear and, frankly, just plain sick.

"Tell him to enter the waters," said the worms.

When Eargon Fooz translated these words for me, I was faced with a choice of fears—my terror of the unknown poisons working in my body, or the fear of what might be waiting in that dark water.

I turned to Pleskit. Taking the sack containing the *oog-slama* from my shoulder, I passed it to him.

He nodded. Neither of us needed to say anything else. He knew that if I didn't come back, I wanted him to take care of it for me.

"Good luck," whispered Linnsy, putting her hand on my shoulder.

"Thanks," I whispered.

Then I stepped into the water.

Instantly hundreds of worms wrapped themselves around my legs and pulled me forward. Within a few feet of the shoreline the bottom dropped off steeply.

I began to scream, but the sound was cut off as the worms pulled me beneath the surface. I struggled to break free, but they held me fast, and no matter how I thrashed and fought, I could not escape.

I did not struggle long. As they drew me deeper into the water, I suddenly heard their voices in my head.

Be still, be still, we will not hurt you.

That alone would have not been enough to keep me still. But at the same time something that looked like a glowing flower with fins swam up to me and pressed itself against my face.

Breathe, thought the worms. *Breathe.*

And I could! That reduced my panic, and I began to relax a little.

Something was glowing in the water beneath me. I nearly gagged when I realized it was a writhing mass of worms—thousands, maybe millions of the things.

Why do you fear us? they asked. Before I could form an answer, they said, *Ah, we see.* Which was the first time I realized that they were not only sending thoughts directly into my mind, they were also reading it. *You have no worms like us on the world from which you came. Oh, we find much conflict in you. And sorrow. Yet strange joy. Goodness, what an odd path you have taken to reach this place!*

They seemed to be forming the words in my own language, though I have no idea how they managed it. *Some of us are hundreds of thousands of years old,* they said, and I realized they were answering my question. *We are millions. We work together with speed and joy. Now be still, try not to think. It distracts us, and we need to check your body.*

So I floated there, deep in the cool, dark

water, a glowing flower covering my face. I was anchored in place by hundreds of worms, some as thick as my thumb, all of them longer than the longest snake that ever grew on Earth.

We have seen this poison before, they said after a while. Then, worriedly, *It is deep within you. It will not be easy, but we can take it out.*

A burning sensation ran through me. I thrashed in the water, but the worms held me tight. I screamed—and was horrified to realize I had driven the breathing flower off my face. I forced myself to hold still—one of the hardest things I have ever done. After a moment it swam back and covered my face again.

All right, said the worms at last. *The poison is gone. At least, the poison of the plants. But you have other poisons we cannot remove, young Tim.*

What do you mean? I thought.

We sense poison in your heart. One poison has to do with the one you call Maktel. Another has to do with your father. These are poisons we cannot remove. Only you can release them. All we can do is warn you. It is not wise to hold such poisons, to nurture them.

*They can eat your heart from the inside out,
hollowing it like a parasite.*

If the worms took any response from me, I
don't know what it was. Emotions, arguments,
sorrows, angers, hurts seemed to be washing
through me in a wild rush, but I could not form
words around them.

I was so caught up in my reaction to what the
worms had said that I did not realize they were
taking me back to the surface until the flower
swam away from my face and I suddenly felt
myself burst into the air.

I heard shouts and applause and turned
toward the shore, which was about five feet
away. Pleskit, Linnsy, and Maktel were waving
and cheering. Eargon Fooz was stomping her
feet on the ground, a huge grin splitting her face.

Suddenly I felt a bubbling in the water.
Thousands of worms thrust their heads into the
air, surrounding me on all sides. They spoke,
and though their words were not in English, I
could understand them—as if they were sending a separate translation into my head while
they spoke aloud to the others.

"We have pulled the poison from your friend.

While in his mind, we learned of what has brought you here. You will not find what you are seeking in the city. However, you may find other things there, things that will be important to your people. More than this we will not say, for it is a place we do not speak of."

The heads waved for a moment, then leaned as one to Eargon Fooz. "You have done well to help these visitors. Stay with them while you can. Do not feel bad when you must leave them. They follow a different path."

The worms propelled me to the shore. I felt as if I was riding a wave.

Pleskit and Maktel reached out, each taking a hand to pull me onto the rocks. When I was on solid ground again I held out my arm to examine it.

The green strands were gone.

I turned and knelt at the water's edge. "Thank you," I said.

"It was our pleasure," replied the worms. "What greater joy could we find than in helping someone else? Travel wisely, young visitor, travel well."

And with that, they disappeared beneath the surface again.

I stood, staring at the dark waters, thinking of what they had said to me.

"Come on, Tim," said Pleskit, putting a gentle hand on my shoulder. "We should get moving again."

I turned to him. With a smile he handed me the pouch holding the *oog-slama*. "Glad you're okay," he said softly.

"Me, too," I muttered as I strapped the pouch back around my chest. I followed him back up the tunnel, thinking about what the worms had said to me about Maktel.

The next two days took us through more strange and beautiful territory. Each hour we traveled, I blessed the fact that Eargon Fooz was with us and guiding us away from dangers, of which there were many. I loved to watch the way the colors on her skin shifted and changed as we walked through the jungle.

I was silent much of the time, thinking of what the worms had said. When we stopped for dinner at the end of the first day, I sat near Maktel and tried to speak politely with him.

He seemed surprised, but later he handed me

half of a fruit that Eargon Fooz had picked for him. It was sweet and juicy.

We had a campfire, and Pleskit and Maktel sang a couple of songs from Hevi-Hevi. Then they had a farting contest. It was in full swing, and getting so hilarious that I had fallen on the ground laughing, when we heard someone approaching.

Immediately we fell silent. Eargon Fooz shifted into what looked like a battle stance.

Then our visitor stepped into the light.

CHAPTER
12
[L I N N S Y]

The Great Urpelli

I almost went out of my skin when Ellico *vec* Bur came limping out from behind that tree and said, "What in the name of Ikthar's beard were you thinking of to run away from our ship on a planet you knew nothing about?"

"We were prisoners," retorted Maktel. "It was our duty to escape."

Ellico looked astonished. Bur looked angry, or maybe disgusted. It was hard to tell with that tiny face. "You were not prisoners!" it screeched. "You were stowaways!"

"You abducted us," insisted Maktel.

"That is the second time you have made that

absurd charge," said the Ellico portion, raising an elegant eyebrow. "Please remember, *you* were the ones who sneaked into *our* ship, and then hid when we came aboard. We most certainly did not want you on this trip, and would have been very happy to get rid of you before we exited Earth's atmosphere if we had had any idea you were on board. Abducted, indeed. What nonsense!"

"You wouldn't take us back," said Maktel firmly. "You kept us locked in a storage space."

"Soft-hearted of us, wasn't it," said Bur, "since by the laws of space we could have flung you into the void."

"You didn't tell us that!" cried Tim, turning to Maktel.

Maktel looked embarrassed.

Ellico *vec* Bur heaved a very human-sounding sigh. "All right, we have decided it is time the four of you understood what is at stake here."

Since they were holding a ray gun, we decided we might as well listen.

"Sit down," said the Trader(s). "This is going to take a while."

We sat—even Eargon Fooz, though she looked terribly confused and distressed.

Ellico *vec* Bur rested one foot on a tree stump covered with curling orange moss, then set the hand holding their ray gun on the lifted knee. The other hand continued to grip the top of their cane.

"Who's your friend?" they asked, gesturing to Eargon Fooz.

She introduced herself.

"We appreciate you taking these four on," said the Ellico portion. "Troublesome as they are, we would just as soon have them survive. Now, as our suspicious young friend here guessed"—they gestured toward Maktel when they said this, of course—"we did not go to Earth simply to discuss the peanut butter franchise with Meenom, or even to pick up our new ship."

"I knew it!" said Maktel triumphantly, looking at the rest of us.

"That was about the only part you got right," snapped Ellico *vec* Bur. Leaning heavily on their cane, they said, "Since you think we are so wicked, why don't you tell us what it is you suspect us of?"

"I . . . uh . . . I don't know, exactly," said

Maktel. "I just had a feeling you were up to no good."

"Well, someone's up to no good," said the Trader(s). "But it isn't us. In fact, both of our stated reasons for coming to Earth were true. We did want to discuss the franchise with Meenom, as a way of reviving our own faltering fortunes. And it truly was a convenient place to pick up our new ship. But these were also covers for our main purpose, which was to investigate some rumors we recently uncovered regarding a plot to disrupt communications all across the galaxy."

"How can that be?" asked Pleskit. "The system has many protections built into it. And what would a plot such as that have to do with Earth, anyway?"

"The uncharted *urpelli!*" gasped Maktel.

"You're on the right track," admitted Ellico *vec* Bur, somewhat grudgingly. "Though we doubt you have any idea yet of its true significance."

"Well, the *urpelli* certainly makes the planet far more valuable than we first thought," said Pleskit.

"The appropriate phrase might be '*infinitely* more valuable,' " said Ellico. "What you have in your sector is not merely an uncharted *urpelli*, which indeed would be a remarkable thing in itself. What you have is something known to exist in only one other place in the entire galaxy."

Pleskit gasped. "Are you saying . . . ?" He stopped, as if he couldn't bring himself to speak the words.

Ellico *vec* Bur finished for him. "We're saying that Earth is located close to a second Grand *Urpelli*—so close that its licensing would be included by law in the Earth franchise."

"And my Fatherly One holds that franchise," murmured Pleskit in awe.

"But you were talking about a scheme to disrupt communications across the galaxy," persisted Maktel.

The reply came from Bur. "Ellico's people like to say that a chain is only as strong as its weakest link. The weak link in the galactic comm system is its reliance on the single known Grand *Urpelli*."

"How weak can it be?" asked Pleskit. "That

urpelli is the most heavily defended thing in the galaxy!"

"Its weakness lies in its uniqueness," said the Trader(s). "The problem is that there is no alternative system—or hasn't been, until now. The speed of the system depends on funneling vast amounts of information through that one bottleneck. If someone could shut down the Grand *Urpelli,* and at the same time provide an alternative—well, the galaxy would be at their mercy."

"And someone is planning to do that?" I asked.

"Precisely. That was what had brought me to Earth."

"So are you, like, a government agent?" asked Tim.

Ellico *vec* Bur laughed. "Hardly! We work for no one but ourselves."

"If what you are saying is true," said Pleskit excitedly, "then Earth is far more valuable than any of us had realized."

"That is stating it mildly," said Ellico *vec* Bur. "The Trader who controls this *urpelli* will become one of the richest beings in the galaxy.

Why do you think you have had such troubles since you arrived on the planet? The few who know about this *urpelli* want control of the planet, and were furious when your Fatherly One managed to secure the franchise. They will do anything to destroy his mission. But that is not the worst of it."

"What else could there be?" asked Pleskit in astonishment.

"What are the five great motivating forces?" asked Ellico *vec* Bur.

"Love, hate, money, revenge, and power," replied Maktel immediately, as if reciting some lesson.

"Precisely," said Ellico *vec* Bur. "And if driving forces are combined, they become vastly more powerful. The desire for money alone would be enough to cause some Trader(s) to move beyond ethical behavior and try to take over this *urpelli*. But for someone with a grudge, a hatred of the Trading Federation, an urge for revenge, a desire for power, a lust for money, and a connection to a powerful group of discontents who would like to overthrow the Trading Federation completely, the goal would be more than simply gaining an incredibly valuable resource. Their intent is broader. They want to control the galaxy."

"The Trading Federation would never let that happen!" cried Pleskit. "They don't like to use force, but they would certainly be willing to use it in a situation like this."

"You would be right," said the Ellico portion of the Trader(s), "save for one thing. These schemers have a brilliant ally named Dr. Limpoc, who has figured out how to *close* an *urpelli*. Not attack it. Not take it over. Simply cause it to cease functioning. And if they shut down the Grand *Urpelli*, then the one near Earth will be the only option to keep the galaxy as we know it running. Since they can threaten to destroy that as well, they will be able, in essence, to hold the entire galaxy hostage. Any attempt to free the *urpelli* from their control will be fraught with the danger that if they are overwhelmed, they will simply destroy it out of spite."

The audacity of the plot left us breathless.

"Why don't you contact the Trading Federation with this information?" asked Pleskit.

Both of the Trader(s)'s faces scowled at this

suggestion. "We are not on good terms with the Federation at the moment. No one in a position of power would believe us even if we did try. We might be tempted to let the plan go forward if preventing this takeover did not represent a matter of enlightened self-interest."

"Who is behind this scheme?" asked Pleskit.

"Well, it's a group of course. But the main player is someone you know well."

They paused, then said something that made Tim and Pleskit cry out in horror.

"Her name is Mikta-makta-mookta."

CHAPTER
13
[MAKTEL]

Pods!

The odor of fear that Pleskit emitted at the mention of the evil hamster-woman who had once tried to drain our brains almost sent me into *kleptra* myself.

"If this information makes you think that Mikta-makta-mookta was a more serious threat than you realized when you first faced her, you would be correct," continued Ellico *vec* Bur. "She is, to be frank, one of the most dangerous women in the galaxy."

"Is Harr-giss involved, too?" asked Pleskit, after he had recovered from his initial shock. Harr-giss had been Mikta-makta-mookta's partner back when she was spying on the Fatherly One.

"That is hard to say. As far as we know, he is still in confinement. Even so, it's possible he has a hand in this plot."

Despite the Trader(s)' explanation, their motives remained unclear, and I still did not entirely trust them. On the other hand, what they had told us fit perfectly with the secret message the Motherly One had given me to carry to Meenom.

"Here is one thing I still do not understand," I said to Ellico *vec* Bur. "Why did you take our side during that debate about whether we should have a party in the embassy?"

Both of Ellico *vec* Bur's faces looked startled. "Because we thought it was a good idea," they said simultaneously.

"It wasn't to cause some sort of trouble?" I asked.

"This wretched childling is even more suspicious than we thought," muttered Bur in disgust.

"And what about that rapid takeoff?" I persisted. "Why were you in such a hurry to get away from Earth?"

"We received an urgent message from our informer that the plotters have accelerated their plan. Our goal was not to escape Earth; it was to intercept a ship carrying a being important to this scheme. Unfortunately, we failed in that attempt."

"I have a question," said Linnsy. "After we pulled you out of the ship, why did you go back in?"

"To retrieve some information we need to stop the schemers," said Bur.

"What kind of information?" I asked.

"That does not concern you, Maktel," snapped the Trader(s), both of them speaking simultaneously.

I got the impression they did not like me very much.

"What happened to the ship?" continued Linnsy. "Did it blow up?"

"No. It is crippled but capable of being salvaged." The Ellico portion sighed. "Such a beautiful little ship. It was very painful to have it crash on its first journey."

"What was that all about, anyway?" asked Tim. "Who attacked us?"

"We're not sure," said Bur, its voice angry. "But it's a good guess that it was someone involved with this plot. The ringleaders are based here, after all. According to my informant, their scheme is set to launch in thirty *kerbleckki.*"

"But that's less than two days!" gasped Pleskit.

"Precisely," said Ellico. "Which means we have to get to the city as soon as possible if we're going to stop this madness. We don't particularly want the four of you tagging along. On the other hand, we don't want you wandering around loose, either, since you might do something to alert them that we're coming. Besides, our friendship with Meenom compels us to protect Pleskit. So we'd better travel together."

"All we need to do is get to the city," said Pleskit. "I can contact any embassy there and they will take care of us."

Ellico *vec* Bur laughed—both parts at once, which made for a weird sound. "You'll have a hard time telling anyone in Ilbar-Fakkam what we're up to."

"Why?" I asked. "Don't they speak Standard Galactic?"

"They don't speak anything," said Ellico. "The place has been deserted for over three hundred years!"

I almost burst into tears. How were we ever going to get home?

"We'll start out at first light," said Bur, "so you'd better get some sleep now. Eargon Fooz, you know the territory. If you would continue to travel with us, we would appreciate it."

"I will go as far as the edge of the jungle," she said. "That is as far as I ever intended to go. My people do not enter Ilbar-Fakkam."

"How come you didn't tell us the city was deserted?" asked Linnsy, her voice bitter.

"You did not ask," said Eargon Fooz, sounding surprised by the question. "You knew of the city and wanted to go there. Since it was built by two-leggers such as you, this made sense—or, at least, as much sense as anything two-leggers do."

"But *why* is it deserted?" I asked.

"We do not know," said Eargon Fooz. "The two-leggers came from another world and built the city. They lived there for hundreds of years without bothering us. Then, one day, they left. We do not go there. Ever."

"All right, that's enough for now," said Ellico *vec* Bur. "Get some sleep. Tomorrow is going to be a hard day."

I slept badly that night, and was the first awake. After a light breakfast, we started out again. Ellico *vec* Bur had been right. The travel was hard. After a while Eargon Fooz again offered to let us take turns riding on her back. This time even I was willing to accept her offer.

Late in the afternoon we were passing beneath a tree that hung heavy with yellowish-orange pods. I was on Eargon Fooz's back at the time. Given our previous experience with pods, I clung close to her neck, not wanting to get near the things. But they had the most enticing smell I had ever sniffed—an odor that seemed to sing to my nose of wondrous tastes, of a treat beyond all others. I found myself looking up in a dreamy way, wondering if these pods might be good to eat. Surely not *all* the plant life on Billa Kindikan was dangerous.

Then I saw a pod hanging so low it was almost inviting me to pluck it. Unable to resist the smell, I stretched up, reaching out my hand.

To my horror, the instant I touched the pod a trio of small, beady eyes blinked open in its skin. It sprouted several long, skinny "arms," grabbed my hand, and plucked *me* instead—dragging me up toward the tree.

My cries of terror alerted the others. I could hear them shouting in dismay.

I screamed again as the pod opened a horrible, fang-filled mouth. It smiled wickedly and drooled on my face. The vines gripped me more tightly, lifting me into the air.

I struggled to break free, kicking and screaming. Other pods sprouted legs and scrambled toward me along the vines, like horrid fat *bypriemm*. That was when I realized that they were not actually attached to the tree. I thrashed wildly, trying to evade their grasp. If I broke loose I would plummet to the ground, but even a bone-breaking fall was preferable to letting these things sink their teeth into me.

Their limbs seemed to be neither arms nor legs, but to function as both. The only sound they made was a wheezy, sucking gasp. They were round and squishy, but that makes them sound less horrifying than they really were. The squishiness meant that they could not be hurt, or at least not easily. Kick or hit them, and it had no effect. Their skin could not be torn.

As I dangled there above the ground, I could see other pods attacking my friends. Then the pod I had tried to pick descended toward me, its mouth wide, its eyes glittering.

CHAPTER
14
[TIM]

Bur's Choice

The podlike creatures crawling over us were terrifying and disgusting at the same time. Their small, beady eyes, their squishiness, their prickly, plastic-like skin, and their terrible clutching limbs . . . even now, sitting here in the detention room of the Interplanetary Trading Federation's court, I shudder when I remember them.

This wasn't the first time I had been in a dangerous situation, of course. But it was the first time I had actually been in a physical fight for my own life, and I found strength and courage I didn't know I had—especially when I saw one of the creatures trying to attach itself to Linnsy's face.

Roaring with anger, I ripped away the two pods climbing up my legs. Then I lunged across the clearing and grabbed the pod attacking Linnsy. I had it around the middle. I started to squeeze, fury giving my grip unexpected power. Its nasty legs curled up, and it fell away from her.

I could hear Pleskit and Maktel screaming and shouting. I turned toward them and saw the Veeblax transform itself into a ferocious-looking head, so scary that two of the pods drew back in terror. Another was approaching Pleskit from behind.

"Watch out!" I cried.

Before Pleskit could turn, I heard a sizzling sound and saw a beam of purple light slice across the attacking pod. It split open, oozing out a thick brownish goo. The smell was horrifying.

Spinning, I saw that Ellico *vec* Bur had whipped out their ray gun. They were standing with their back to a tree, zapping the horrible pods, which fell to the ground with their legs curling and twitching whenever the ray hit one. With Ellico's other hand the Trader(s) were

slashing around them with their cane, beating the pods aside like so many incoming soccer balls. Fierce anger contorted their faces.

Eargon Fooz, too, was fighting savagely. Her voice like a trumpet, she reared back, stamping the vicious pods beneath her feet. Several were attached to her back, and I plunged toward her to help pull them away. But the pods had obviously spotted the Trader(s) as the greatest menace, because suddenly they all let go of the rest of us and began to surge toward Ellico *vec* Bur. They looked like a living carpet of coconuts scuttling across the jungle floor.

The Trader(s) fought valiantly, using one hand to lash out with their cane, which they used almost like a sword, and the other to fire the ray gun. I wanted to get in and help, but with their ray gun sizzling this way and that, I couldn't get close. Despite the ray gun, several pods managed to grab on to the Trader(s). Others clustered around their feet. Suddenly Ellico *vec* Bur fell backward. I heard the Ellico portion shout in anger, or maybe pain, then a strange shriek of despair from Bur. The sound shivered down my spine.

Even though they were down, the Trader(s) continued to fire. The stink of sizzling pods filled the air. Then, suddenly, the two dozen or so that were left scuttled back into the trees, retreating in the same eerie silence with which they had attacked.

We rushed to Ellico *vec* Bur, who had undoubtedly saved all our lives. I choked back a cry of horror. The Ellico portion of the Trader(s) was severely wounded, his elegant clothing torn, his face and hands oozing blue blood.

"Help him!" cried Bur's tiny voice. "You must help him!"

To my surprise, it was Maktel who hurried to the Trader(s)'s side.

"I had emergency medical training in Wilderness Way," he explained quietly as he began to work over Ellico *vec* Bur's body.

The Ellico portion remained silent. Bur, however, began to wail, a horrible keening that shivered up and down my spine.

Finally Maktel turned and said softly, "It's very serious. He won't be able to travel. We need to find someplace to shelter them."

"The area has some caves," said Eargon Fooz.

"We might be able to find one where they will be safe."

"Good," said Maktel. "I'll stay with Ellico *vec* Bur while you go look for a cave. Maybe one of the rest of you should stay, too—so I'll have help in case there's another attack."

"I'll stay," Pleskit said.

"Bad idea," Linnsy said. "That would leave Tim and me with Eargon Fooz, and neither of us can speak her language."

That was when I noticed that Linnsy's leg had been hurt in the attack. "Why don't you stay?" I suggested. She started to object, but I pointed to her leg and said, "Looks like it might be hard for you to walk anyway."

She hesitated, but then agreed that it was probably the best idea. As Pleskit, Eargon Fooz, and I went to look for a cave, I glanced back and saw Linnsy gently taking the ray gun from Ellico *vec* Bur's hand. She sat down on the ground next to Maktel, cradling the ray gun and staring nervously into the trees.

Following Eargon Fooz, Pleskit and I pushed our way through the jungle. It was dark, the blue sun mostly blocked by the huge trees that stretched above us. I was twitching with nervousness, wondering what vicious plant might be waiting to attack at any moment. Weird cries echoed high in the treetops. I looked up, trying to catch sight of the creatures that made them, but could see nothing but the dense ceiling of foliage. Once, off to the right, I saw a pair of large green eyes. But they blinked shut the moment I spotted them, and the creature, whatever it was, disappeared.

We were lucky to have Eargon Fooz with us. She knew the territory and had a good sense of where to look, so it didn't take as long as I would have thought to find a cave.

It was Pleskit who spotted it. "Look," he said, grabbing my elbow. "Over there." He was pointing to a small hill, barely visible through the thick foliage. "See?" he asked. "That dark spot . . . off to the right."

"Looks promising," said Eargon Fooz (according to Pleskit's translation), and we began beating our way toward it.

The spot was perfect, a dry cave that went nearly twelve feet into the hill with no sign that Ellico *vec* Bur would be sharing it with any kind of man-eating critter.

Quickly we made our way back to our friends, who were plenty happy to see us, let me tell you.

"No problems while you were gone," reported Linnsy.

"But some scary noises," said Maktel. "I kept thinking things were gathering to attack."

"Let's get Ellico *vec* Bur to that cave as quickly as we can," I said, feeling more nervous than ever.

But that was easier said than done, since the Trader(s) were too weak and wounded to walk.

"We can use something else I learned in Wilderness Way to handle this," said Maktel. Then he showed us how to lash together some branches to make a travois—a simple job made more complicated by fear that any branch or vine we tried to cut might strike back!

When the travois was ready, we carefully placed the Trader(s) on it and dragged them to the cave. Bur complained all the way about the bumpiness of the ride. I might have found that really annoying, except it was clear the little creature was only trying to protect its partner.

Once we reached the cave, we faced a new question—namely, what to do next?

"We can't just wait here for someone to find us," said Linnsy.

"No, you have to go on," said Bur, startling me when it broke in on the conversation. "Setting aside the fact that no one will be looking for us here anyway, we've got to get to the city to deal with the threat to the communication system."

"We?" asked Pleskit.

"You cannot go alone," said Bur. "You don't know the way, or what to do when you get there."

"But you can't travel now," protested Linnsy.

"Ellico cannot travel," corrected Bur. "I, however, must. The fate of the galaxy depends on us stopping Mikta-makta-mookta's plot." It paused, then added, "That means that one of you will have to act as my host. Any volunteers?"

I stared at Bur in astonishment. The mere thought of letting that crablike thing crawl onto my head and stick its legs into my ears made me shudder with horror.

After a long silence Bur said angrily, "All right, if none of you will volunteer, I'll have to choose for myself."

Removing its right *tweezik* from Ellico's ear, it pointed at one of us and said, "I want *you*."

CHAPTER

15

[LINNSY]

Me, Myself, and Bur

When Bur pointed at me, I felt a coldness seize my stomach. The idea of letting that crablike *thing* climb onto my head and attach itself to my brain was more horrifying than anything I had ever imagined.

I saw the others staring at me, their faces shifting from awe to pity to horror.

"Why Linnsy?" demanded Tim, asking the question I had not been able to get past the sudden dryness that had sealed my throat.

Ignoring Tim and looking directly at me, Bur said, "You were the one who tried to help us when we were injured on the ship. We can sense your empathy and your open mind, which are necessary for a successful meld. Besides, you are the most mature of your group."

"Hey!" said Tim, as if to protest. But I could tell he didn't really mean it. The funny thing was, I had been teasing him for years by calling him immature. Now I would have given anything to be the least mature person here.

"I cannot force you," continued Bur. "The meld would never work if you were to resist. But you must understand that without my guidance it will be impossible for you younglings to do what must be done."

"You know I cannot go into the city with you," said Eargon Fooz sadly, as if to reinforce Bur's point. "You will be on your own once I leave you at the edge of the jungle."

I swallowed hard, trying to will my throat to open up so that I could speak.

Tim moved closer to me. "Linnsy, you don't have to—"

"No," I said, finally finding my voice. "That's the point, Tim. I *do* have to. We can't just stay here and let Mikta-makta-mookta take over the galaxy." I looked directly at Bur. Bowing my head slightly, I said, "I accept your offer."

Bur closed its eyes, and its tiny voice twisted out a cry of pain as it pulled the second *tweezik* from Ellico's ear. Despite the fact that Ellico was still unconscious, he cried out, too—a terrible sound, so filled with loss and sorrow it almost made me weep.

As Bur clambered awkwardly down to the floor of the cave, I noticed that Ellico was bald, something it hadn't occurred to me to wonder about when he had had a permanent attachment on his head. I wondered if he had always been bald, or if having Bur there had somehow removed his hair—or had it been tentacles, like his beard?

What is this going to do to my hair? I wondered. Part of me was disgusted by the vanity of the thought; what was my hair compared to the fate of the galaxy? Another part couldn't help but wonder what I was going to look like the next time I saw Jordan.

I could tell from Bur's slow, painful movements that it was not used to moving on its own. The sound of the creature's claws as it dragged itself across the cave's stony floor made me shiver. I felt I should offer to help, to pick him up. But my fear and revulsion left me mute, which made me ashamed.

At last Bur reached my side.

I stood still, trying not to scream as the crablike creature attached its claws to the side of my right leg and began to climb. When it reached my waist, it shifted around to my back. I could feel its tiny claws pierce the skin on either side of my spine. Each place the claws jabbed in immediately went numb, as if Bur were injecting some kind of anesthetic—almost like a bee sting in reverse.

I tried to stand still as Bur climbed my spine, but I could not stop the fearful trembling that shook my body.

Bur reached my neck, then climbed directly onto my head. I felt as if its claws were digging through the thin skin that covered my skull, going straight to the bone. The shell of its body was hard, but not cold.

"Calm, calm," murmured Bur. "Stay calm or this will not work. The more you fight me, the more it will hurt."

It settled around my head, its sides expanding, adjusting, then closing again to make a tight fit. I flinched as the edges clamped against my skull, just above my ears.

"Calm," repeated Bur. "Calm. Relax."

I took a deep breath and tried to hold still as Bur's *tweezikkle* probed the side of my head, searching for my ears.

Suddenly they found the openings and thrust in. I felt a blaze of pain as they formed the connection to my brain.

Then everything went black.

CHAPTER
16
[TIM]

Fallen Comrade

When Bur settled onto Linnsy's head, she started to shudder. Suddenly her eyes rolled back so that nothing but the whites were showing. The shuddering grew more violent. A scream ripped out of her—a terrifying scream that echoed horribly in the cave.

"Stop!" I cried. I lunged toward her, ready to rip Bur from her head.

Pleskit grabbed my arm. "You must not interrupt," he said urgently.

"Let me go!" I shouted, struggling to get away from him. *"Let me go!"*

It was Linnsy who stopped me. Her scream

123

ended as abruptly as it had begun. Her face twisted and twitched and then, suddenly, relaxed. She looked so surprised and happy, it made me almost as nervous as when she had been screaming. Putting out her hands to motion me away, she said softly, "It's all right, Tim. I'm fine."

"How do I know that's you talking, and not Bur?" I asked.

"It's both of us," she replied, which gave me a little ripple of fear. "We are one now."

Bur, perched atop her head, was smiling. I found the sight of that smug face revolting.

I turned to Pleskit.

He nodded. "As far as I know, Linnsy *vec* Bur are speaking the truth."

Somehow Pleskit speaking her—*their*—new name like that made the whole situation more real, and I shuddered at the words. Pleskit put his hand on my arm. "Tim, you must remember that Bur is a symbiote, not a parasite. This new being is a partnership."

"We need to go now. We have delayed enough." Though the words came out of Linnsy's mouth, I wasn't sure if by "we" she meant all of us, or just her and Bur.

"What about Ellico?" asked Maktel.

Tears welled up in Linnsy's eyes. "We must leave the former partner. He will understand. We will seek aid for him."

She seemed oddly confident of the things she was saying. Not that Linnsy had ever lacked confidence. But now she was—well, it seemed as if she had decided that she was going to be the leader, and there was no doubt that the rest of us would follow her. Them.

Ellico stirred on his bed of leaves. "Linnsy *vec* Bur are right," he said, his voice soft and weak. "You can do nothing for me here. I will be all right on my own."

We all knew he was lying, that he would not be all right. We could only hope he would survive long enough for us to get help.

"If it will set your minds at ease," said Eargon Fooz, "after I accompany you to the edge of the jungle, I will come back here to watch over your comrade. I am not a healer. But I can at least try to guard him from attack."

"We are most grateful," said Linnsy *vec* Bur. She walked to Ellico's side, knelt beside him, kissed him gently on the forehead. Whether the kiss was supposed to be from her or from Bur, I could not tell.

Maybe there was no way to tell them apart now.

"We'll need this," said the Linnsy portion of the *veccir*, as they reached down and took the ray gun from Ellico's side. They tucked it into their belt then turned and strode from the cave.

Maktel, Pleskit, and Eargon Fooz followed. I was the last to leave, though I'm not sure why. I stood in the entrance, looking back at Ellico.

"Go," he said, when he realized I was still

there. He waved a blue hand to send me on my way. Then his bald head dropped back and his eyes closed.

Still I stood watching him.

"Go," he whispered again, his voice fierce. *"Now!"*

I turned and ran, clutching the *oog-slama* to my chest.

The day was hot. The jungle smells were so rich and thick they almost made me dizzy. I noticed that Eargon Fooz stopped several times and pulled lengths of vine from the base of certain trees. She bit them off with her strong teeth, then coiled them in her hands.

It made me nervous to see her messing with *any* vines in this killer jungle, but I figured she knew what she was doing. I did wonder *why* she was doing it, just exactly what she was up to. But I was far too concerned about Linnsy to worry about it very much. It took two or three hours before I finally got up the nerve to talk to Linnsy . . . to Linnsy *vec* Bur.

"So . . . how're you feeling?" I asked.

"The Linnsy half of us feels better than it

ever has," they answered. "The Bur portion is mourning for its fallen comrade, but enjoys the excitement of having a fresh mind to merge with."

"Is this, uh, *permanent?*" I asked.

"Bur would never force someone to be its partner," they answered.

I looked skeptical.

"We know that you are thinking that is simply the Bur part of us speaking," said Linnsy's mouth. "But you have to understand this goes both ways, Tim. The Linnsy part has access to all of Bur's knowledge and memory." Her mouth smiled. "Here's the good news, Tim. You were right about the galaxy. It's wider and stranger and more wonderful than any of us back home imagined. Well, maybe any of us but you. The Linnsy part of us almost wishes that you had been the one Bur chose, because you would so much love to find what we are finding as our memories merge. Some of it is scary—more than the Linnsy part wants to know about life right now. But it's exciting, too. Exciting and wonderful, and she would not trade it for anything."

I stared at her, having no idea what to say.

Then a new question hit me like a hammer. If we ever did get out of this mess, would Linnsy be coming home with us—or was she now a citizen of the galaxy?

And if that was the case—what was I going to tell her mother?

CHAPTER
17
[PLESKIT]

Farewell to a Friend

I watched Linnsy *vec* Bur uneasily as we traveled through the jungle, wondering if their transition into a joined being had been as simple and complete as Linnsy seemed to think. From stories I had heard from the Fatherly One, I knew that some new *veccir* feel a surge of excitement when their brains first mesh, but later have a reaction of fear and sorrow over the loss of individuality. I told myself that surely Bur knew this as well, and would be guarding against it, or know how to deal with it should it happen.

Late that afternoon we came to a clearing in

the jungle with an enormous orange stone on one side.

"Ah," said Linnsy *vec* Bur, "we know where we are now. We can lead the way from here, Eargon Fooz." Though they were speaking through Linnsy's mouth, it was obvious the knowledge came from the Bur portion of the partnership.

Eargon Fooz linked her fingers, then pulled them apart, her people's gesture of parting. "Your willingness to go on alone is a relief to me," she said. "I was growing uneasy about venturing this close to the city. I will leave you here, and wish you the best of luck." Turning to Linnsy *vec* Bur, she added, "I will return directly to your fallen comrade and protect him as well as I am able."

"Thank you," said the Bur portion of the new being. The Linnsy portion, however, looked troubled. I was troubled, too, when I figured out what that look meant: Linnsy was torn between her concern for Ellico and her fear that if he did live, Bur would leave her to return to him! It was clear she was moving deeply into the *vec* union.

Maktel stood before Eargon Fooz and bent his head until his *sphen-gnut-ksher* was pointing at the ground, a sign of deep respect and humility. "I was suspicious of you at first," he said. "And I do not think that it was wrong to be cautious. But you have proven a good and worthy friend, and we owe you our deepest thanks."

Eargon Fooz smiled and put her hands on his shoulders. Then she threw back her head and made a high-pitched warble that was oddly beautiful.

The next farewell was mine. I was truly sorry to see our friend leave us, and told her so. But I think Tim was sorriest of us all. "You saved my life by taking me to the worms," he whispered, putting his hands on her long neck. "Thank you."

I translated his words for Eargon Fooz. She smiled. "The best way to thank me is to use that life wisely. Here, I have a gift for you."

She handed him the vines she had been collecting and coiling as we walked.

"It's a rope," she said. "You may find it useful."

"Thank you," said Tim, obviously startled.

Eargon Fooz bent to put her arms around him,

and they embraced tightly. After a moment she released him, then turned and trotted away, the shifting colors of her skin causing her to disappear among the purple foliage mere seconds after she had left us.

I felt downhearted at saying farewell to the friend who had helped us so much. Much as I hate to confess it, I had been comforted by having an adult with us. As I thought about that, I realized Linnsy *vec* Bur was actually half adult, or contained a full adult unit, or something like that. But it was hard to hold the idea in my mind when I looked at the *veccir* and saw, mostly, the same Linnsy I had met the first day of sixth grade—the same, yet utterly different because of the strange creature clamped tightly onto her head.

Toward evening we reached the top of a hill that overlooked the city. The scene was quite beautiful, a symphony of spires and domes lit by beams of light that played over it in lovely patterns.

"What happened to it?" I asked. "Why is it deserted? And why are there so many lights— why any lights at all—if it is deserted?"

"No one knows," said Bur. "Ilbar-Fakkam has been empty for hundreds of this planet's years. But all its systems continue to function, as if the city is simply waiting for its people to return. It's a very strange place—but a good spot for beings who are up to no good to hide in."

"It's hard to imagine why anyone would leave this place," said Tim as we started down the hill. "It looks so wonderful I feel like I've died and gone to sci-fi heaven. Of course, being deserted does make it easier for us just to walk in. I had been worried about the way Linnsy and I were going to stick out here."

"What an *ango-dabbik*," muttered Maktel.

I shot him a nasty glance. But he was right: It was an amazingly naive comment, at least from our point of view. It struck me again how different Tim's life had been from mine, how differently we understood the universe.

To my surprise—but surprising only because I was still not accustomed to what she had become—it was Linnsy *vec* Bur who explained the situation.

"Tim," they said gently, speaking through Linnsy's mouth, "even if the city was fully pop-

135

ulated, why do you think you or I would look any stranger to its residents than Pleskit or Maktel? As long as they were already in contact with other planets, we would appear as just one of the many possible variants of intelligent life."

Tim blinked, then actually laughed. "Boy, do I feel like a bonehead!" He looked at the city again, then shuddered. "It's kind of like one of those ghost towns from the Old West, only about a million times bigger. It's going to feel weird just walking in."

"Actually, we're not going to walk right in," said Linnsy *vec* Bur.

"We're not?" I asked.

"No. We're going through the sewers."

CHAPTER
18
[MAKTEL]

The Sewers of Ilbar-Fakkam

I felt a shudder of revulsion when Linnsy *vec* Bur told us we would have to enter the city through its sewers.

Clearly Tim felt the same way. "If the place is deserted, why the heck do we have to sneak in?" he asked, sounding as if he had been tricked.

"The city may be empty, but the building where Mikta-makta-mookta has set up her headquarters is protected by some very serious security equipment," said Bur. "We believe our best chance to approach it undetected is to go through the sewers. However, trying to enter the sewer from the city itself would also attract attention. So we need to start from outside the city."

"Why don't we just go into the city and wait until night to lift a manhole . . . uh, *being-*hole . . . cover and sneak into the sewers that way?" asked Tim. "Less time to spend down there that way."

Linnsy *vec* Bur shook her head, an Earthling gesture that made me feel more confident the Linnsy portion was still active. "Access to the sewers from inside the city is not as simple as you think, Tim. You're still operating from an Earth model. We'd need a security code to get into one of those openings—either that, or we'd have to blast our way in, which would definitely attract more attention than we want."

"What kind of attention are we going to attract in a deserted city?" asked Tim skeptically.

"We told you, the city's systems are still working. Repair 'bots and security 'bots would be there in minutes. Sirens would probably go off. Mikta-makta-mookta and her crew would be sure to know something was going on."

"I take back what I said about sci-fi heaven,"

muttered Tim. "This is more like a sci-fi night-mare!"

While they were discussing this I was worrying about something else—namely, the possibility that the Bur portion of Linnsy *vec* Bur was only helping us break into the schemers' command room for some selfish reason of its own. I feared that when we got there, we might meet with some terrible surprise, and I was a little disgusted by the simpleminded trusting of the others, who were so glad to have Bur along that they were almost drooling with thankfulness.

Was I the only one who had the presence of mind to be suspicious?

The question plagued me all through our walk to the edge of the city.

As we traveled, the moon rose behind the city—a lonely single moon, much like the one on Earth, though vastly larger than that moon. The towers of Ilbar-Fakkam stretched high in the darkening sky. Small winged creatures flitted through the night, shrieking as they passed within inches of our heads.

Given our experiences in the jungle, I found this terrifying.

"Fear not," said Linnsy *vec* Bur, speaking through the Linnsy portion. "They won't bother us."

I started to ask how they could be sure, but realized that Ellico *vec* Bur had undoubtedly studied the planet before we crashed here. And what Ellico *vec* Bur had studied, Linnsy *vec* Bur now knew.

We circled a quarter of the way around the city, heading for the river that ran alongside it. I was stumbling with exhaustion by the time we came to the place where we could enter the sewers. The city was built on a bluff that rose about a hundred feet above the river and—precisely where Linnsy *vec* Bur had said we would—we came to a deep chasm. Above it, about halfway to the edge of the city, we could see an opening in the side of the cliffs where water was trickling out.

"Well, I guess if the city is deserted, the water won't be *too* ooky," said Tim, looking up at it. "Where does it come from, anyway? I mean, it's not like there's anyone in there flushing the toilets."

"Sewers are meant to carry away rainwater as well as waste," said Linnsy *vec* Bur. "Also, there are automatic systems in the city still circulating water for various reasons." They looked at the chasm. "It's unfortunate we can't cross here. It would make things easier. Well, one does what one must. Onward, friends."

We began climbing the embankment; the rocky slope was smooth and very steep, but not impossible.

"You'll have to be careful when we go in," said Linnsy *vec* Bur just before we reached the top. "There may be some strange things living inside."

Tim, who had gone up to the opening, pulled back. "What kind of strange things?"

"You never can tell, can you?" said Linnsy *vec* Bur with a smile on both their faces. Then they stepped in front of Tim and led the way into the dark tunnel that we hoped would let us save the galaxy.

CHAPTER
19
[TIM]

In the Sewers

Dim lights flickered on overhead, almost as if sensing our presence. I jumped in surprise, even though I should have expected that the sewer for this city would be considerably more high-tech than on Earth. Still, it was eerie to think that the lights had been put there by beings who had abandoned the city hundreds of years before.

I quickly realized that traveling through the sewer wasn't going to be as disgusting as I had feared. This was partly because a ledge ran along the side, about fifteen inches above water level. It was also partly because the city was deserted. Rather than wading through a swamp of alien poop, we were walking slightly above a broad flow of dark water.

The sewer itself was about ten feet high and about fifteen feet across. The walls—so smooth they felt as if they were made of some sort of plastic—rounded gently into the ceiling without ever forming a corner. A cross-section of the sewer tunnel would have been shaped more like an egg than a box.

The journey went smoothly for the first several minutes. In fact, things didn't start to get nasty until we heard something splashing in the water next to us.

"What's that?" I asked nervously.

"Could be anything," said Bur. "I'd suggest you stay as close to the wall as you can."

"If I get any closer, I'm going to qualify as wallpaper!"

The problem with keeping so close to the wall was that it slowed us down. As we inched along, I kept gazing down at the water, trying to figure out what might be lurking beneath the surface. But the light was too dim to see anything other than the occasional ripple.

About fifteen minutes in we came to a branch in the sewer, a place where two tubes joined to form the one through which we had been traveling. (Or, considering it from our side, a place where the tunnel split.)

Linnsy *vec* Bur called a halt while they considered which way we should be going. I got the impression they were having a conversation, even though they were standing in complete silence. When Bur had first chosen Linnsy, my reaction had been relief. Now, for the first time, I felt a flicker of jealousy as I wondered what it would be like to have an alien being linked to my brain, feeding me information.

I got so involved in thinking about Linnsy that I wasn't paying as close attention to the water as I should. All of a sudden I heard a splash, the loudest yet, then felt something grab me by the leg. I looked down and screamed. A thick green tentacle had wrapped itself around my leg. It started to pull me toward the water. I grabbed for the walls, but their smooth surface gave me nothing to hold onto.

"Help!" I screamed.

Pleskit grabbed one of my arms. Maktel grabbed the other. Within seconds I felt as if I had become the rope in a game of tug of war. While Maktel and Pleskit gripped my arms, the tentacle was pulling me toward the water with powerful strength. I was stretched out above the surface of the sewer, my body angled downward.

Another tentacle snaked out of the water and grabbed my other leg.

"Hold on to me!" I cried.

Suddenly I heard a sizzling sound. A beam of light sliced through the first tentacle, and then the second. The water frothed as the now stumpy tentacles withdrew. Pleskit and Maktel hauled me back onto the ledge.

The ends of the tentacles, now oozing green goo, were still wrapped around my legs, thrashing like a pair of demented snakes.

"Get them off!" I cried, in near hysterics. *"Get them off!"*

"Don't touch them!" ordered Linnsy *vec* Bur. "They may be poisonous." The *veccir* edged past Maktel on the ledge and, using the ray gun on a different setting, carefully sliced off the tentacles.

145

They fell into the water below. We saw a sudden froth of activity, and then they disappeared. I couldn't tell if they had swum off on their own or if something had grabbed them to eat.

"How did you know how to do all that?" I asked, once I was able to talk at all.

Linnsy *vec* Bur shrugged. "What's the point of having a symbiotic partner if you can't work together?" they asked in unison.

Then the Bur part chuckled, which sent a little chill down my spine.

They knelt to examine my legs. "It's a good thing you were wearing pants," they announced, speaking through Linnsy. "They protected you from any skin damage." She paused, and I could tell she was communicating with Bur. "We're not sure if you should take them off to avoid the possibility of any poison soaking through, or leave them on to protect you in case of another attack."

"I'll leave them on," I said hastily—then wondered if I was making a stupid mistake just to keep from walking around in my underwear.

"We thought you would," said Linnsy *vec* Bur. "All right, let's get moving again."

146

"Which way are we going?" asked Pleskit.

"We have to cross over to the other side."

"You've got to be kidding!" squawked Maktel—and the only reason *he* said it instead of me was because he got the words out faster. I was so shocked by the idea that I couldn't speak at first. I just pointed at the water going, "But . . . but . . . but . . ."

"We have to go up the tunnel on this side for another quarter of a mile," said Linnsy *vec* Bur. "We can cross there, then walk back down this way."

As we walked, my legs began to itch. I couldn't tell if it was because some poison from the tentacles had soaked into my pants, or because my imagination was making me feel that way. I knew my imagination *could* do that to me, because once I got some fleas on me at a friend's house. Even though we got them all off before I went home, for the next three days every time I thought about it, I kept feeling fleas again.

Knowing that didn't stop me from being worried sick. But the worry wasn't enough to get me to take my pants off—especially since it was always possible another of those tentacles might come snaking out of the water and grab me. I wanted to be sure I had something covering my skin in case that happened. Besides, I was *not* walking around in my underwear!

Finally we made it to the crossing spot.

"You expect us to climb over on *that?*" squawked Maktel.

CHAPTER
20
[L I N N S Y]

Perilous Crossing

We were not surprised by Maktel's reluctance. The method for crossing the sewer was nothing but a series of recessed bars, about an inch thick and four inches long, that went up the side and across the ceiling of the sewer tunnel. Bur pulled an image from his mind to share with me, that of the group of native inhabitants who had built the city. They had strong, tentacle-like fingers and could scurry up one side of such a wall and down the other without the slightest fear of slipping.

Obviously, this was not the case for our group.

It is hard, in writing this, to describe the way

the Bur portion of our mind worked with the Linnsy portion. It is not as simple as talking to one another. Thoughts were often shared instantly, in a way that went beneath and beyond words. Speaking together, we said, "We will use the rope Eargon Fooz gave Tim to bind ourselves together. If one of us falls, the others will be able to pull that one quickly from the water—or perhaps even hold *yeeble* from striking the surface."

"It's a terrible idea," said Maktel.

Bur spoke our response for us: "We can leave you here if you would prefer."

"I'll go," said Maktel grimly. He turned to Tim and Pleskit and said, "If I die and you live, please tell my Motherly One what happened."

"I foresee a future for you in drama," said Bur. "In the meantime, let's get to work."

To our surprise, despite his reluctance, it was Maktel who was most capable when it came to linking us together with the rope. "I learned it in Wilderness Way," he said, speaking without a trace of smugness. We found this almost as surprising as the knowledge itself.

Thus linked, we started our climb. Tim

objected to us going first, but we reminded him he was speaking to Linnsy *vec* Bur, not just Linnsy, and that we were the leader and the adult in the group.

"Well, one of you is an adult, I guess," said Tim grumpily.

"Even if you take the average of our ages, we are almost elderly by Earthling standards," we told him. Then we started up the ladder.

The climb up the side was not terribly hard. It was when the wall began to curve into the ceiling, so that we were climbing at an angle, that things got tricky—and even more difficult when we actually reached the ceiling. We realized that by hooking our toes under the crosspieces, we could support ourselves better than if we were just dangling by our hands.

The dark waters beneath us appeared tranquil. Even so, we knew that death lurked below the surface. Our arms grew tired. Though the Bur portion of ourselves could feel the pain, it was also able to act as cheerleader, urging us to hold tight, to be strong.

Pleskit was second in line, followed by Maktel, then by Tim. Though we did not say it out loud, the reason we had chosen this arrangement was that we thought Maktel was most likely to fall, and we hoped that if he did, Tim and Pleskit would be able to keep him from plunging into the water.

The other choice would have been to put Maktel second, and here we made a cold-blooded decision to minimize the risk to ourselves. We made this choice not out of fear, but because our knowledge was the necessary key to completing our task.

We had just reached the point where the wall began to curve back down, and were realizing how tricky it was going to be to descend head-first, when we heard a cry of despair from behind us. Tilting our head back we were able to see through Bur's eyes that Maktel's feet had slipped, and he was dangling from the ceiling by his hands.

"Tim! Pleskit!" we shouted, using both our voices together. "Hold tight! Tim, move back a little. That way if Maktel falls, the rope will be tighter and hold him higher above the water.

Things did not improve when we saw a pair of tentacles come wriggling out of the water.

They reached up searchingly, as if attracted by the sound. Tightening our right hand's grip on the rung, curling our toes to hold ourselves more firmly in place, we took out our ray gun. The shot was difficult, because we had to use Bur's sight line and Linnsy's hand to make it, and we had not had time to completely coordinate ourselves. The Linnsy portion felt a terror that we might miss and strike one of the boys. But the tentacles were reaching higher. Maktel, having seen them, was squirming in terror, which increased his danger of falling. We had to act.

"Hold still!" we cried, using both mouths.

Then we fired.

We heard a satisfying hiss as our ray sliced the tentacles in half.

"Maktel, see if you can swing your feet back into place," we shouted. "No! Do not *see* if you can do it. DO IT!"

He seemed to respond to the firmness of the order. To our relief he managed to get first one and then the other foot hooked back into the rungs.

That was . . . difficult, thought Bur, speaking only in our head.

Once we had made it down the far side, we quickly untied the rope from our waist and wrapped it around one of the rungs. That way if the boys fell, they would not pull us in. Also, we would have something to brace against to pull them out—though whether we could get them out before the tentacled creatures grabbed them was anyone's guess.

Fortunately, we did not have to try. A few moments later we were all standing together again.

The triumph in the boys' faces was good to see, and we all embraced one another. But there was little time for celebrating. Moments later we were working our way back toward the fork in the system.

About an hour later we came to the exit our informant had told us would lead to the citadel of the conspirators.

"Won't it be locked?" asked Tim.

"No. Access spots to the sewers are locked from the outside, to prevent anyone from sneaking in. But they can always open from the inside, to prevent workers from being trapped. This exit opens onto a shaft that will lead us into the basement of the building where the plot is being run."

"How do you know all this?" asked Maktel, suspicious as usual.

"We are operating on information we received from a contact inside the conspiracy. That was why Ellico *vec* Bur went back into the ship after you had dragged them out—to retrieve this information—though they hardly suspected that it would be Linnsy *vec* Bur who ended up using it. Now come along."

It took but moments for us to leave the sewers and climb into the subterranean levels of the building housing the conspiracy.

We needed to move with greater caution now. Though we knew that Mikta-makta-mookta did not have a large crew here, we didn't want to do anything to alert them to our presence.

Slowly, patiently, we made our way from floor to floor, sometimes using the slide-ramps, sometimes a stairwell, twice traveling through air shafts that our informant had told us about—though in both those cases Maktel was so terrified that it was hardly worth the effort, since the noise of his protests probably offset any secrecy we had gained.

Our plan was to get to the twentieth floor, which was where Mikta-makta-mookta had established her headquarters. Once there, we would try to get a sense of where things stood.

The plan was derailed when Pleskit tapped us on the shoulder.

Turning, we saw a huge being holding Tim in the air. This being had four hands. One was clamped over Tim's mouth, the second wrapped around his waist, the third and fourth tight around his neck.

"I think you should come with me," said this monster. "I think you should drop your gun and come very quietly with me. Very quietly. I am very fast. This boy's neck is very slender. It would not be wise to do anything to make me nervous."

CHAPTER
21
[TIM]

Captured

The hulking giant who captured me had moved with astonishing silence for someone so huge.

I had been following along behind Linnsy *vec* Bur and the others when, out of nowhere, I felt myself snatched into the air. I struggled, of course, but it was pointless. My captor was fantastically strong. Besides, I was afraid with him holding me so tightly that if I fought too hard, I might hurt the *oog-slama*.

He continued to move with silence, speaking only when he needed to tell the others where he wanted them to walk. He never let go of me, never loosened his grip, never seemed to feel an instant of strain from carrying me.

With the others following, he carried me to an elevator. Soon we reached the top floor of the building.

The entire floor was a single huge room, lavishly decorated. I wondered if the art on the walls, the carvings on the ceiling, were some remnant of the people who had built the city, or if they had been brought in by Mikta-makta-mookta.

In the center of the room, looking completely out of place, stood several high-tech walls of blinking and flashing instruments.

Standing in front of one of those panels, studying a dial, was our old enemy Mikta-makta-mookta.

My terror and despair were complete.

She turned shortly after we came in. Her face raced through a series of emotions—shock, anger, and then, finally, pleasure. And why not? She had us at her mercy.

"Oh, well done, Gorjac!" she cried. "Well done indeed!"

She walked closer to us, and the anger

returned to her face. Whiskers bristling, furry cheeks twitching, she snarled, "Is there no place in the galaxy I am safe from you interfering little *gnerfs?*"

"Probably not," said Linnsy *vec* Bur.

Mikta-makta-mookta's nose twitched in contempt. "And you, Bur—what an astonishing thing to find you perched on an Earthling's head! When did you decide such a creature was worthy of your partnership? Are you sure you won't reconsider? It's not too late for you to rejoin us."

I looked at Bur in shock. Had Ellico *vec* Bur been part of Mikta-makta-mookta's scheme after all? Suddenly Maktel's wild suspicions no longer seemed so absurd.

"Ellico *vec* Bur ended their connection with your group as soon as they found out what you and Dr. Limpoc were really up to," said the Linnsy portion of the *veccir.* She spoke with confidence, but I couldn't help wondering if that confidence came from the fact that her mind and Bur's were merged, so she could say for sure what happened, or because Bur had taken control, and was lying through her lips.

"Who's Dr. Limpoc?" I asked.

"Shut up," said Mikta-makta-mookta. At the same moment a tall being—lean, green, and very scaly—stepped from behind a gleaming wall of instruments and dials.

"I am Dr. Limpoc," he said, flicking out his tongue and licking his eyebrow.

"Get back to your work, Limpoc," snapped Mikta-makta-mookta.

"As you wish," he said humbly, bowing his head and licking his eyebrow once again.

"Since you've met Dr. Limpoc, you might as well know that he is the scientist who figured out just how we can close down the Grand *Urpelli*. He's quite brilliant, if not entirely socially acceptable."

"We see," said Bur. "Limpoc has no social ability. You have no ethics. And Gorjac here is obviously lacking in the brains department. Is being seriously deficient in some important skill a key requirement for joining your little club?"

Mikta-makta-mookta's furry face twisted with contempt. "Take them away, Gorjac," she snarled. "I'll deal with them later."

Gorjac grunted. His hands still tight about my neck, he carried me out of the room.

We went to a room one floor down. Gorjac waited until the others had entered, then flung me in and slammed the door. I landed on my back, bruised and terrified and trying not to cry. I cradled the *oog-slama*, hoping desperately that it was all right.

Linnsy *vec* Bur knelt beside me. "We are sorry," they said, speaking with both their voices. "We have failed you."

It was the longest night of my life—made longer by the fact that Mikta-makta-mookta came to see us a few hours later to brag about what she had in store for the galaxy.

She was guarded, of course, by her giant protector, Gorjac. Because he had been holding me from behind, this was the first time I got a good look at him, and I was more terrified than ever to realize that I had been in his grasp. His shoulders had to be at least a yard wide. His head was oddly small for his size. He wore only a pair of tight black pants. His lemon-yellow skin was covered with swirling tattoos.

"I brought this clock for you," said Mikta-makta-mookta, her nose twitching with self-delight as she placed a large brown object on the floor. "I've set it so that you can follow the countdown with me. We have eight *kerblecks* to go," she said, pointing at the glowing signs on the face of the clock. I assumed they were numerals, though I couldn't read them.

"Don't worry, Tim," she said, turning to me as if she understood my confusion. "Your friends will explain to you how to read the clock. When the countdown is finished, I will initiate Dr. Limpoc's process for freezing the Grand *Urpelli*." She smiled her evil hamstery smile. "It will be interesting to see how long it takes before genuine panic seizes the Trading Federation. I think I'll give them a few days. Once their fear has had a chance to fully ripen, the leaders will receive a message I prepared some time ago, telling them that I have discovered an alternate Grand *Urpelli* and that I will be glad to license it for their use."

"My Fatherly One holds the license for that area!" said Pleskit defiantly.

Mikta-makta-mookta chuckled. "Such an innocent! My message will also stress that if anyone dares to thwart me, I will destroy the new *urpelli* the same way I did the old one. I will be perfectly happy to plunge the galaxy into chaos. However, I do not think this is something the galactic leaders will want to take a chance on."

She chuckled again, a horrid cheebling sound. "You know, in a way I'm glad you younglings are here to see this. Given all the trouble Pleskit and Tim have caused me, it seems fitting in a way. In fact, I think I'll have Gorjac bring you up to the main room when it's time to launch our little project. I want you to witness the beginning of the end!"

She left, slamming the door behind her.

We stared at one another glumly.

"This is horrible!" cried Maktel. "What are we going to do?"

At first no one had an answer. Then I felt the *oog-slama* wiggle against my chest. I looked down—and whooped in astonishment.

It had become a Veeblax!

If not for the fact that a mad hamster-woman was about to take over the galaxy, I would have been ecstatic.

The new Veeblax crawled onto my shoulder and closed its eyes. In its resting form it looked basically identical to Pleskit's Veeblax when it was not imitating something—which is to say, somewhat lizardlike. The only real difference was that mine was a bit smaller.

I kept looking from my Veeblax to Pleskit's. Something was nagging at the back of my brain.

And suddenly I had it.

"I think I've got an idea," I whispered. (I would have shouted, but I was afraid the room might be bugged.)

The others gathered close to me, and I explained what I had in mind.

"You're crazy," said Maktel.

"Or at least far more tricky than we would have guessed," said Bur approvingly.

I remembered that Pleskit's Fatherly One was fond of saying, "Tricky is good."

"Do you think it will work?" I asked eagerly.

No one knew. But since no one had any better idea, we decided to try my plan.

It took most of the night to get ready for it, and for some of us the preparations were very painful.

But by morning we thought we had a chance to save the galaxy.

CHAPTER
22
[PLESKIT]

Battle for the Galaxy

Gorjac came to fetch us about fifteen minutes before Mikta-makta-mookta was scheduled to give Dr. Limpoc the "Go" signal for freezing the Grand *Urpelli*. It was not lost on any of us that the *urpelli* would be used to deliver the signal that would begin its own destruction.

Gorjac wasn't alone this time. He had three guards with him, all of them carrying weapons. One guard for each of us. Obviously Mikta-makta-mookta was taking no chances.

The giant looked us over and shook his head, as if he couldn't believe a group of kids—well, three kids and a *veccir* who was half-kid—could be worth all this bother. We lined up in front of him, Linnsy *vec* Bur, Maktel, Tim still wearing his *oog-slama* pouch, and me with a Veeblax on my shoulder.

He didn't bother to look behind the door. Why should he?

"Put these on," he growled to Maktel and me. He handed us a pair of pointed caps made of some shiny black material. Obviously the caps were designed to shield our *sphen-gnut-ksherri* so they could not blast him. They strapped under our chins and were very humiliating to wear. I felt like a clown, though I did not feel like laughing.

Once we had the caps securely in place, Gorjac and friends marched us out of the room and up to the next floor.

Mikta-makta-mookta was waiting for us at the door, playing the role of gracious hostess. "I am so glad you could come!" she cried, doing a wonderful job of faking delight. "I was afraid you might not be able to make it. That would have been so sad. I've prepared the most lovely surprise for you."

The words made me nervous, since we had

been hoping to surprise *her*. Had she figured out our plan?

Then we stepped into the room and saw her "surprise": standing at the side of the room were Ellico and Eargon Fooz.

Neither of them looked good. Ellico was haggard and filthy, his elegant clothes torn, his face a mask of tragedy. Eargon Fooz looked terrified. I felt certain it was because when she was dragged here into the city, she had violated her people's powerful taboo against coming to this place.

Clearly, Mikta-makta-mookta had us all in her power. I hoped she would take plenty of time to gloat over it. Time was something we needed.

My enemy didn't let me down. She launched into a long tirade about how angry she was over the first two times Tim and I had thwarted her plans, explaining that as soon as she was done taking over the galaxy, she was going to sit down and have a nice long think.

"I'll need a fair amount of time," she said, smiling happily, "because I want to figure out the *best* way to make you suffer."

As we stood listening, we looked frightened and sad, just as we were supposed to. When it looked like she might stop bragging and threatening and actually get on with her project, Linnsy *vec* Bur got her going again by asking, "How did you get Ellico and Eargon Fooz?"

Good, I thought. *Keep her talking.*

"Why, I'm glad you asked," said Mikta-makta-mookta. "It wasn't that hard, actually. When I saw that Bur was here, I knew there was a good chance Ellico would be somewhere nearby—though whether he was alive or dead, it was hard to say. Dead, I assumed, since it was hard to imagine Bur detaching from him if he were not. But I needed to be sure. So I sent Gorjac out looking for him. It's not that difficult to follow a trail if you have some genetic markers and the right technology. Gorjac has told me the path you took to get here; I must say I'm impressed at your resourcefulness. He found your friends, of course, and escorted them back here so they could be part of the big event—though that poor native creature Eargon Fooz seems to have been traumatized by being forced to enter the big, bad city. Wherever did you children find her, anyway? Well, never mind. We're all together now, and that's what counts. I do love an audience when I'm about to launch a takeover of the galaxy. Dr. Limpoc, are you ready?"

She paused, then laughed, a high chittering sound. "Oh, dear—silly me! I forgot. Dr. Limpoc had some last-minute qualms about what we were about to do, and we had to have him locked away for the morning. You know how these eccentric geniuses can get. Ah, well—I'll just have to pull the lever myself. Shall we have a countdown? That would be fun, don't you think?"

My disgust for Mikta-makta-mookta was growing deeper by the moment. I wondered if she was purposefully trying to goad us into reacting so she could have the pleasure of squashing us.

I also wondered if the last element of our plan was in place yet.

Mikta-makta-mookta went to one of the blinking control panels. In the center of the panel was a lever, bright red, about two feet long.

"You know, it won't be very spectacular at first," she said, sounding apologetic. "I mean, when I pull this lever, you won't see or hear anything that indicates that within two weeks the galaxy will be groveling at my feet. But that's the way it is—once I pull the lever, there's no turning back. The Grand *Urpelli* will be, as you Earthlings like to say, toast! Now, count with me. Ten. Nine. Eight."

None of us was counting. She stopped, looking very displeased.

"The lady said to count with her," rumbled Gorjac, sounding a little like a volcano that was about to erupt.

She started again.

We counted with her: "Ten. Nine. Eight."

I wondered when Tim would give the signal, wondered, for a moment, if he was too afraid to give it, if I should do it instead, and wondered if, in doing so, I would ruin everything.

"Seven. Six. Five."

I counted with the rest of them, but I was so tense I was afraid my *sphen-gnut-ksher* would erupt inside the protective shield and sizzle my own skull.

As we intoned "four," Mikta-makta-mookta flexed her arms as if getting ready to pull the lever.

"Three."

Tim, I thought. *Tim!*

"Two," we said in unison.

"NOW!" cried Tim.

At his signal Linnsy ripped the Veeblax, which had been masquerading as Bur, from her skull. She flung the creature at Mikta-makta-mookta, who screamed in rage. Her rage turned to frustration as the Veeblax wrapped itself around her head, shaping itself into a kind of hood that completely blinded her.

The Veeblax on my own shoulder—which, of course, was really Tim's new Veeblax—shrieked in delight at the show.

Gorjac, roaring in fury, grabbed for Tim. But Tim had thrown himself to the floor and was crawling away, as per our plan.

At the same moment Maktel and I stripped off the caps that had been shielding our *sphen-gnut-ksherri.* Searing purple energy sizzled out from both our heads, throwing our guards into *kling-kphut,* much as I had done to the wretched Jordan during the first week of school.

That left one more guard, and the fearsome Gorjac.

Dropping our previous plan, I hurried across the room to try to free Ellico and Eargon Fooz.

Tim was scrambling for the door. Gorjac turned to go after him, then turned back when Mikta-makta-mookta, who was desperately trying to pull the Veeblax from her face, screamed for him to help her.

Tim flung open the door. I was relieved to see that Bur had managed to make its way up to this floor. I heard a cry from Ellico. Was it relief, terror, joy? I could not tell.

Tim snatched Bur from the floor and started across the room.

Gorjac had turned toward him again. Maktel sprinted across the floor and leaped onto the giant's back. Gorjac, roaring in astonishment, spun around, trying to dislodge Maktel. It was all the time Tim needed. He rushed forward with Bur and slapped the creature onto Gorjac's back.

Bur sunk its pincers into the flesh around Gorjac's spine. This time it did not merely anesthetize the flesh, as it had done when climbing Linnsy's back. Injecting the full force of its venom, Bur soon had Gorjac stumbling and staggering across the room. Inch by inch it climbed the giant's spine. With each inch it went up, the giant's roars grew weaker.

Just when it looked like the battle was over, three more guards burst into the room. They had their ray guns drawn, but the confusion was so great they weren't sure what to do, where to fire. I had managed to free Ellico and Eargon Fooz by that time, and the two flung themselves into the fight. They headed straight for the newcomers, Eargon Fooz rearing and shrieking a ferocious battle cry, Ellico staggering forward, weak and wounded but with a look in his eye that would have stopped me in my tracks from sheer terror had it been directed at me.

The guards fired. Purple light shot across the room. I heard the sizzle of flesh, but Ellico and Eargon Fooz kept moving forward.

Linnsy was wrestling with Mikta-makta-mookta, holding her paws and trying to keep her from hurting the Veeblax. Tim and Maktel dangled in the air as they clung to Gorjac's mighty fists, trying to keep the stumbling monster, weakened but still strong, from reaching behind him to pluck Bur from his back.

Another inch, another, and then Bur reached the giant's skull. It thrust its *tweezikkle* into Gorjac's ears. I heard an electric crackle, then Gorjac screamed and toppled forward, landing flat on his face.

Ellico and Eargon Fooz were locked in hand-to-hand combat with the new guards that had rushed in.

I rushed to Linnsy's side to help her with Mikta-makta-mookta. The Veeblax had leaped off by this time, terrified by the pummeling it had taken. Mikta-makta-mookta and Linnsy were wrestling on the floor, Mikta-makta-mookta trying to crawl forward to throw the big switch, Linnsy trying desperately to keep her from doing so. I raced forward and flung myself on top of the evil hamster woman. A moment later I felt Tim, and then Maktel, land on top of me.

We had her pinned.

"Well," said Bur's scratchy voice, sounding tired but triumphant. "That would seem to be that."

And it was.

Almost.

CHAPTER
23
[LINNSY]

The Final Choice

Picking up the pieces after that terrible battle was not easy. The four of us holding down Mikta-makta-mookta didn't move, didn't dare let go of her, for fear she would bolt for the panel and throw that switch. So we couldn't get up and see to our friends' wounds, or even be absolutely certain our enemies were completely out.

Most of that work fell to Eargon Fooz, who was delighted to see the rope she had given Tim—and that had been taken from him when we were captured—hanging from Gorjac's belt. She sang to herself as she used it to bind Mikta-makta-mookta so tightly that she couldn't move.

It was a relief to be able to get up and walk away from her, though once we were off her, she started a stream of horrible cursing. I wanted to stuff something in her mouth to shut her up, but I was afraid she would bite me if I did.

The guards, a little less dangerous than Mikta-makta-mookta, we bound with their own clothing.

Then, at last, we felt free to care for our own wounded. We four kids were bruised and battered, but didn't seem to have broken any bones, which was a minor miracle.

Pleskit's Veeblax was bruised and battered, too, from the pummeling Mikta-makta-mookta had given it while trying to pull it from her face. The poor little critter whimpered as Pleskit took it into his lap, whispering, "Well, pal, looks like you just saved the galaxy!"

"Looks like we all saved the galaxy," said Maktel, who had a bright green bruise on his face that seemed to be the Hevi-Hevian equivalent of a black eye.

Tim's new Veeblax was clinging to his leg, gleeping desperately.

I was glad they were all safe. But there was someone else I needed to see desperately. That was Bur, of course, who had become as close to me as my own skin in the days that we had been joined, who knew my every secret, and in whose mind I had found a trove of memories and experiences that I could share so fully it was as if they had actually happened to me—a life story beyond my wildest imaginings that had become partly my own.

When Tim had suggested Bur and I separate, so the Veeblax could imitate Bur and take its place on my head with the hope that we might take Mikta-makta-mookta by surprise, my first reaction had been complete panic. And after everyone—including Bur and me—had decided that this was our best chance, I had endured a pain unlike any I had ever known when Bur separated from my skull.

Now I had a new pain to face: Would Bur go back to Ellico, or would it want to stay with me? If my new partner wanted to return to Ellico, how could I stand the pain of losing it?

But if it wanted to return to me, what would that mean for the rest of my life?

Part of the question was solved for me—which might have been a relief, except it happened in the worst possible way. When I went to retrieve Bur from Gorjac's head it released that small skull with a shudder, saying, "That is the emptiest brain I have ever been connected to!"

We went together to Ellico's side.

Eargon Fooz had pulled the Trader to the wall and propped him up. But it was clear to both Bur and me that Ellico was dying, and equally clear that there was nothing we could do about it.

The others gathered around us. I know the boys felt a sense of sorrow and loss. Here, after all, was someone we had thought to be an enemy but who had helped us survive—whose aid in that final, terrible battle may well have saved us all. He was a friend, a comrade, but, for one of us, so much more.

That one, of course, was Bur. And the loss my new partner felt as his old partner was dying was a pain so searing it was almost beyond imagination.

I set Bur gently upon Ellico's chest. It climbed slowly, laboriously, onto the Trader's head.

Ellico stirred, opened his eyes. Looking at me, he said, his voice weak, "You were a good match for Bur. Will you take care . . . take care . . ."

His voice trailed off.

The wail of despair that tore out of Bur, an anguished cry of sorrow and loss, made my knees buckle and I fell to the floor, gasping. Instinctively I put my hands out to Bur. It clambered off Ellico's head and into my arms. I lifted it to my head, and felt a surge of relief when it settled back into place, recreating our union.

Do you want me to stay? it asked, speaking in my head, speaking to me alone.

I realized then that Bur would leave me forever if I asked it to. And part of me wanted that—wanted to be free of its constant presence, free to return to my old life at school. But the thought of that freedom also left me with a feeling of desperate aloneness.

And how could I go back to sixth grade when I had tasted the freedom of space through the memories that Bur shared with me?

Do you WANT to stay? I asked.

We do not like to move, it replied.

That was not the question, I thought back, a trifle snappishly.

I felt a wave of amusement. *A life with you would be . . . different . . . than the one I have been used to.*

I fear that you will be bored, I thought.

I fear that you will be restless, Bur replied. *You have much to learn yet of your own world, your own people. But will you want to stay on Earth to do that when you are sharing my memories of so many other places, so many other sights?*

No.

Then what are we to do?

Who owns the spaceship?

We do.

Can it be repaired?

It can.

It seemed almost too daring to think of leaving Earth—and yet so impossible to think of going back.

I did not know what to say, to think.

We have time before we must choose, said Bur.

It was right.

After we used Mikta-makta-mookta's equipment to contact the authorities, we had a three-day wait before officers of the Trading Federation arrived to retrieve us. Messages were sent to Earth and to Hevi-Hevi, to reassure our parents.

Because the possible consequences of Mikta-makta-mookta's plan were so horrifying, we were taken to Trader's Court to tell all we knew about what had happened. I have spent the last several days writing down my part of the story.

Bur has been with me all that time, of course.

Those sentences could as easily read: "We have spent the last several days writing down our part of the story. We have been together all that time, of course."

Tomorrow we hand our depositions to the judge.

Then Bur and I must decide whether we will stay together, or separate.

CHAPTER
24
[TIM]

Our Separate Ways

I am writing this after all the rest is over, to explain what happened after Maktel, Pleskit, Linnsy, and I gave our depositions to Judge Wingler. I think I'm actually going to miss this room. It's going to seem strange going back to Earth.

The judge decided we hadn't done anything wrong, of course. In fact, we were all given medals, in honor of our efforts on behalf of Galactic Civilization. They even made one for Ellico, something Bur says would have made him laugh.

Our parents were brought to the celebration,

which was kind of neat. I mean, how often does a guy get an award like that?

The hard part came when the ceremony was over and it was time for the partings.

Maktel's Motherly One insisted on taking him straight back to Hevi-Hevi. I was astonished to realize that I was actually going to miss him. We even hugged each other goodbye.

Pleskit's Fatherly One had come, too, of course. As usual, he was angry with us for getting ourselves into such trouble, yet proud of how we had gotten out of it and, in this case, pretty much saved the civilized galaxy in the process. He was also distracted by the fact that the existence of the second Grand *Urpelli* so close to the planet for which he held the Trading Franchise meant that he was teetering on the edge of becoming the richest being in the galaxy.

My mom had come along with him, and she was a mess, emotionally speaking. She was so relieved to find out that I was all right, so angry that I had gotten into this mess to begin with, so proud of my being honored by the Trading Federation, not to mention so excited about going to another planet herself—"I've never even been to Europe" she kept muttering—that she finally stole my line and kept saying, "I think my head is going to explode!"

Eargon Fooz had come to Trading Central with us. Even more exciting, she had requested permission from Pleskit's Fatherly One to come back to Earth with us for the time being, since she could not go back to her own people for at least a year because she had broken the taboo and gone into the city.

"That's silly," I said when I heard about it. "It's not like you *wanted* to go into the city. You were abducted!"

"That has nothing to do with it," said Eargon Fooz glumly. "I have been in a bad place, and I am unclean. My people will not let me come back yet. It would be dangerous for all of them."

"What about your children?" I asked.

"The village will care for them, just as they would if I had died. And, indeed, this is like a little death. I shall miss them. They will miss me. But in time we will be together again."

I still thought it was stupid, but my mother

took me aside and told me there are some things you really can't argue with people about. Which may or may not be true, but I decided to let it go for the time being.

Actually, I was pretty excited at the idea of Eargon Fooz coming back with us, because I thought she was so cool, though I wasn't sure what she would think of Earth—or Earth of her, for that matter.

And then there was Linnsy.

My old pal Linnsy.

Linnsy *vec* Bur, to be more precise.

This isn't easy to write.

Linnsy is not coming back with us.

It's so weird. I was the one who always wanted to go into space. Now Linnsy is the one who's gone.

Needless to say, her mother and father are not amused. They came here to Trader's Court as well, and they were pretty shocked to find that their daughter had become a *veccir*.

"I feel like you got married or something!" cried Mrs. Vanderhof in dismay.

Bur is certainly not what the Vanderhofs had in mind for a son-in-law. On the other hand, it could be worse. They could have ended up with Jordan!

I didn't say that out loud—which may be a sign that I'm getting smarter.

The night before Linnsy *vec* Bur left, they came to my room to say goodbye.

"I can't believe you're going away like this," I said, trying not to cry.

"How can Linnsy go back to what she was?" they asked, speaking with both their voices at once.

I didn't answer.

They leaned forward, and Linnsy reached out to take my hands in hers. "Listen, Tim," she said, speaking with only her own voice. "I know things now that I didn't know before. The truth is, I know more than I wanted to know yet—stuff about being an adult. It's all stuff I wanted to know eventually, I guess. But I sure didn't need to know it this soon." She paused, then said, "I want you to do something for me when you go back to Earth."

"What?"

"I want you to take Misty aside and talk to her."

I snorted. "Next to Jordan, Misty is the kid in our class least likely to listen to me. She thinks I'm cornstarch."

"Tell her you're bringing a message from me," insisted Linnsy.

I sighed. "All right, what is it?"

"Tell her . . . tell her Linnsy says not to be in such a hurry. Tell her all the stuff about growing up is exciting and interesting and she's going to be glad to get to it. But tell her this, too—"

Linnsy paused, and I saw tears in her eyes. "Tell her that once you know it, you can't *not* know it ever again. You can get there any time you want. But once you're there, you can't go back. Tell her I said there's no hurry."

I nodded, not sure of what to say. "Is that it?" I said after a while. "Any other messages you want me to deliver?"

"Tell the class I said goodbye."

"What about Jordan?"

"Just tell the class I said goodbye." She leaned over and kissed me on the forehead. "See you around, Tim," she whispered. "Try to stay out of trouble."

Then she gave me a little punchie-wunchie.

After Linnsy *vec* Bur left I sat in my room for a long time, not moving.

Tomorrow morning we leave for home— Mom and I, Pleskit, his Fatherly One, Mr. and Mrs. Vanderhof, and Eargon Fooz.

I'll be glad to get back to Earth.

But somehow I don't think Earth—or sixth grade—will ever seem the same again.

A Glossary of Alien Terms

Following are definitions for the alien words and phrases appearing for the first time in this book. Definitions of extraterrestrial words used in earlier volumes of *I Was a Sixth Grade Alien* can be found in the book where they were first used.

For most words we are only giving the spelling. In actual usage many would, of course, be accompanied by smells and/or body sounds.

The number after a definition indicates the chapter where the word first appears.

A complete glossary, covering the extraterrestrial words used in all eight volumes of *I Was a Sixth Grade Alien*, can be found at:

www.bruce coville.com

ango-dabbik: stupid person, one who does not think clearly. Literal translation: "bonehead" (17)

bypriemm: a rodentlike creature found in the northern wampfields of Hevi-Hevi. What makes them especially dangerous is their ability to charm hapless travelers by appearing cute and friendly. As soon as the intended victim is lulled into complacency the *bypriemm* latches on and sucks the life out of its victim, growing hideous and bloated in the process. (13)

gortzwump: a nourishing but vile gelatinous substance, this "food" has inspired countless jokes by stand-up comedians across the galaxy, as well as at least 4,500 tall tales. First created on the planet Gortz, it has been credited with saving millions of lives in emergency situations. "And at least ten of those beings are glad they survived," is the standard response whenever this figure is cited. (4)

ikbu: A declaration of peaceful intent. The word can be used as a question or as a statement. Standard Galactic. (8)

kerbleck: (plural: *kerbleckki*) 87.4938 Earth minutes. A Standard Galactic measure of time, used for convenience when beings from different planets are discussing how long something might take. (7)

phwooper: A lie or untruth. The word is slightly slangy, and is generally reserved for occasions when the person telling the *phwooper* has not merely fibbed but has stretched the truth well past the breaking point. (4)

tweezik: (plural: *tweezikkle*) A nerve-rich appendage through which several varieties of intelligent symbiotes are able to make the connection with their *vec* partners. *Tweezikkle* come in many shapes; generally they are hard-shelled and look somewhat like a leg or a claw. A typical *tweezik* has more nerve fibers than a human spinal cord. Most *tweezikkle* have special—and quite delicate—fibrous tips that are used to make the neuron connection to their partner-beings. (4)

About the Author and the Illustrator

BRUCE COVILLE, the author of more than seventy-five books for young readers, was born in Syracuse, New York. He grew up in a rural area north of the city, around the corner from his grandparents' dairy farm, where he often dreamed of traveling to other planets. His favorite writers included Hugh Lofting, Eleanor Cameron, and (a little later) Edgar Rice Burroughs.

In the years before he began to make his own living as a writer, Bruce worked as a gravedigger, a toymaker, an elementary-school teacher, and a magazine editor (among other things). Now he mostly writes, but also spends a fair amount of time traveling to speak at schools and conferences. He also produces and directs unabridged recordings of fantasy novels for children.

Bruce and his wife, Katherine, live in an old brick house in Syracuse, which they share with a number of strange animals and whichever of their three children happens to be home at the moment.

Bruce's best-known books include *My Teacher Is an Alien*, *Goblins in the Castle*, and *The Skull of Truth*.

TONY SANSEVERO received his art education from Boston's Massachusetts College of Art. He has illustrated several picture books and teen novels, and is an award-winning fine artist as well. He lives in Syracuse, New York, with a menagerie of weird animals and his collection of sci-fi toys.